BLESSED ARE THE PEACEMAKERS

A
Shattered Nation
Novella

By
Jeffrey Evan Brooks

Dedicated to my darling Evelyn Anne.
A little book for my little princess.

This is a work of fiction.

ISBN: 1495935795

ISBN-13: 978-1495935794

Published by CreateSpace Independent Publishing Platform

Cover art by Meredith Scott

Acknowledgements

As was the case with *Shattered Nation*, this book would not have been possible without the help of family and friends who thoughtfully offered their critiques and suggestions. In particular, I'd like to thank my wonderful sister Meredith for again offering her artistic talents to create the cover art.

I'd like to thank William C. Davis, one of the best Civil War historians working today and author of the definitive biography of John C. Breckinridge, for answering my questions and clearing up a serious misunderstanding I had about Breckinridge. Had he not done so, I would have made an embarrassing mistake in the writing of this novella.

I'd also like to thank R. E. Thomas, a whiskey expert in addition to being a fellow writer of alternate history and author of the delightful book *Stonewall Goes West*, for giving me some very useful information about the state of whiskey in the 1860s.

Finally, I'd like to extend my gratitude to the fine people who regularly post in the Alternate History Discussion Board at www.alternatehistory.com. They've always been a valuable sounding board for my ideas, even if some of them have rather unusual political notions and an odd obsession with the Byzantine Empire.

Above all, I would like to thank my wonderful wife Jill. Her constant support and assistance has been absolutely crucial. Whether by her own reading and editing or by her simple encouragement, she has made these books possible. They wouldn't have been written without her.

Message from the Author

The unexpected success of *Shattered Nation: An Alternate History Novel of the American Civil War* has been a source of enormous satisfaction for me. *Blessed are the Peacemakers* is the first of what I expect will be several novellas that follow on from *Shattered Nation*. It is intended to serve as a bridge between *Shattered Nation* and its sequel, *House of the Proud*, which I hope to publish in late 2015 or early 2016. I'm also doing preliminary work on a novel detailing what happened in the Shenandoah Valley during the events of *Shattered Nation*. It's become increasingly clear to me that the literary adventure I embarked upon when I started work on *Shattered Nation* some years ago will be a lifelong project.

Yet it won't be the only project. Although I find the American Civil War utterly fascinating and absorbing, it is far from my only historical interest. Indeed, I am one of those unfortunate people who are interested in so many different things that they find it difficult to focus on any one subject for a long amount of time. When confronted with occasional writer's block with *Shattered Nation* or *Blessed are the Peacemakers*, I have distracted myself by doing preliminary work, mostly researching and outlining, on alternate history dealing with the Second World War, the United States during the 1790s, the reign of Henry VIII, and the last years of the Roman Republic.

Alternate historical fiction is an immense and surprisingly untapped source of literary possibilities. Though I am still comparatively young, the sad truth is that I doubt I will live long enough to write all the books I want to write.

Writing *Blessed are the Peacemakers* has been an interesting intellectual adventure. As with any excursion into the realm of alternate history, it's fascinating to look at the events of the past from a different perspective. The outcome of the American Civil War and the subsequent course of American history, like most other major historical events, has the whiff of inevitability about it. But nothing in history was inevitable. Had events of the American Civil War unfolded as depicted in *Shattered Nation*, the situation in 1865 would have obviously been vastly different than what it was in the history with which we are familiar. Trying to map out the course history might have taken, while being careful not to be carried away by flights of fancy, is a tremendously difficult yet strangely satisfying task.

Composing the actual text of the treaty, which appears at the end of the novella, was especially challenging and enjoyable. I spent many hours scouring through the texts of eighteenth and nineteenth century treaties of peace and commerce in order to master the proper language. This might strike some people as unimaginably boring, but I personally found it to be quite fun.

I hope you enjoy this little volume and I hope you look forward to what's coming in the future.

Dramatis Personae

Confederate Delegation

Secretary of War John C. Breckinridge

Vice President Alexander Stephens

Congressman William Miles

Postmaster General John Reagan

Union Delegation

Secretary of State Horatio Seymour

Former Vice President Hannibal Hamlin

Major General John Porter

Attorney General Jeremiah Black

British Army

Colonel Garnet Wolseley

"A peace may be so wretched as not to be ill exchanged for war."

Tacitus

"Blessed are the peacemakers, for they shall be called the children of God."

Matthew 5:9

Chapter One

The beautiful vessel glided gracefully south down the Cape Fear River. On each side of the river, forts and batteries fired their cannon in salute as the ship passed by. As it approached the entrance to the ocean, people on small boats and pleasure craft waved their hats and raised cheers, just as the crowd on the dock at Wilmington had done when they had departed two hours before. Everyone knew that it was not an ordinary ship, nor was it setting out on an ordinary journey. The frigate *CSS Shenandoah*, the pride of the Confederate Navy, was carrying the Southern delegation to the conference that would, it was devoutly hoped, create a treaty of peace between the Union and the Confederacy.

The crewmen of the *Shenandoah* sweated profusely in the summer heat, yet they went about their business in a jaunty and playful manner, singing songs as they worked the ropes and scrubbed the deck. Officers shouted orders and encouragement while Captain James Waddell stood on the poop deck towards the stern, his hands clasped behind his back, overseeing operations as though he were an all-powerful monarch. The wind was strong, filling the sails and making the use of the steam engine unnecessary.

Strolling the deck near the bow was a tall, well-built man with whiskers that cascaded off his face like a waterfall and compassionate blue eyes that shone with intelligence. John C. Breckinridge, one of the four men chosen by President Jefferson Davis to represent the Confederacy at the peace conference, chatted amiably with some of the sailors and observed their activities with genuine interest.

As the ship neared the point where the Cape Fear River emptied into the Atlantic Ocean, the enormous citadel of Fort Fisher, which had defied the mightiest warships of the Union Navy, came into view. As the *Shenandoah* sailed past, the fort's garrison fired off their cannon in a final salute and gave three cheers. Captain Waddell ordered the guns of the frigate to fire their own salute in response and the crewmen gathered on the port rail and rigging to wave their hats and cheer their landlubber comrades. It all brought a smile to Breckinridge's face. The sailors and soldiers were warriors to a man, but they were all celebrating the prospect of peace.

At long last, the *Shenandoah* turned to port and entered the Atlantic Ocean. Anxious to make good time, Captain Waddell ordered steam to be raised and before long a tall pillar of black smoke was bellowing out of the ship's smokestack. With the sails full and the engine operating well, the ship increased its speed as it turned north to begin the long voyage to Canada.

Breckinridge continued to pace the deck, allowing himself the luxury of reflecting on his own long voyage which had brought him the deck of the *Shenandoah*. He was the scion of one of Kentucky's most distinguished political families. His great-grandfather, the Reverend Jonathan Witherspoon,

9

had been a signer of the Declaration of Independence. His grandfather, John Breckinridge, had introduced the famous Kentucky Resolutions in the state legislature in 1798 and served as Attorney General of the United States under Thomas Jefferson. His father Joseph had served as the Speaker of the Kentucky House of Representatives.

Coming from such an illustrious linage, great things had been expected of John C. Breckinridge from the moment of his birth. He did not disappoint.

Breckinridge's legal career had begun well, though his sensitive temperament prevented him from ever serving as a prosecutor. After coming back from the Mexican War, he had been elected to the Kentucky State Legislature and gone on to win a seat in Congress in 1851. He had become known for his intelligence, clear-headedness and sense of honor, while building a reputation for maintaining personal friendships despite political differences. His rise had been meteoric. In 1856 he had been chosen as James Buchanan's presidential running mate. With the victory of the Democratic ticket in that year's election, Breckinridge had become the youngest Vice President in American history.

In 1860, the Southern pro-slavery faction of the Democratic Party had nominated him to run for President against Abraham Lincoln. Breckinridge had privately found this ironic. Though he carried the banner for slavery, and though much of his support had come from secessionist radicals, he was actually a moderate on the questions of slavery and secession. He supported the constitutional right of the Southern states to secede from the Union, though he thought secession unwise and unjustified. He publicly supported the institution of slavery, but admitted when in the company of close friends that it was immoral and destined to eventually disappear. For better or worse, though, Breckinridge believed that the Constitution protected slavery

10

and that the federal government had no right to interfere with it. He had owned a few slaves over the course of his life, though by 1860 he had owned none.

During his days as a Kentucky lawyer, Breckinridge had represented free blacks in court and become a supporter of the project to emancipate slaves and resettle them in Liberia. Two of Breckinridge's uncles were active abolitionists and, many years before, Breckinridge had been a subscriber to *The North Star*, the abolitionist newspaper printed by Frederick Douglass. It seemed strange that fate had called him forward to defend slavery when he himself felt so ambivalent towards it.

Breckinridge had not been surprised when Lincoln had overwhelmingly defeated him in the election, for he had never expected to win. His candidacy had been a forlorn hope. Lincoln's victory had led to the secession of the South, the creation of the Confederacy, and the subsequent War for Southern Independence. Breckinridge had remained in Washington representing Kentucky in the Senate even after Fort Sumter had been fired upon and the first great battle had been fought at Bull Run. However, his repeated assertions that secession was constitutional and Lincoln's war measures were illegal had led to his denouncement as a traitor. To avoid arrest, he had fled to the Confederacy in the fall of 1861.

Upon his arrival in the South, he had exchanged the suit of a politician for the uniform of a soldier. He had been placed in command of a brigade of Kentucky Confederates, soon to become legendary as the Orphan Brigade. He had gradually worked his way up through the ranks, becoming a major general and seeing action in many of the bloodiest battles in both the Western and Eastern theaters. Although unschooled in the military arts, he had proven himself an unusually gifted and innovative commander, earning the respect of both his friends and foes. Already a popular

11

politician throughout the South before the war, his military achievements had raised Breckinridge to the level of a hero.

After the defeat of Lincoln in the 1864 presidential election and the unofficial ceasefire which followed, President Davis had summoned Breckinridge to Richmond to join the Cabinet as Secretary of War. In that capacity, he had bent himself to the task of improving the flow of food and supplies to the troops and preparing the army for either demobilization or renewed fighting. In May, President Davis had selected him to be one of the Confederate commissioners to the peace conference. It had been a long journey to the decks of the *Shenandoah* as it set forth on its voyage, but it certainly had not been uninteresting.

Breckinridge was so enmeshed in these thoughts that he almost didn't notice the approach of Congressman William Porcher Miles, a dapper-looking, bearded man in his mid-forties. Breckinridge turned as he sensed his approach. Miles gave him some quick, hard pats on the shoulder, beaming a great smile.

"A pleasant day, isn't it, John?"

"It is, William. And not just because of the weather."

"That's the truth. Amazing, isn't it? To be chosen for such an honorable task as this?"

"Blessed are the peacemakers, eh?"

"Quite so. I feel rather like Franklin, Adams, and Jay must have felt when they began their negotiations for peace with the British after Yorktown."

Breckinridge smiled at Miles's boyish giddiness. He had known Miles slightly in Washington before the war, when he had been Vice President and Miles had represented South

Carolina in the House of Representatives. Prior to that, Breckinridge knew, Miles had been the Mayor of Charleston, where he had achieved some distinction through his inventive reform of the police force. His passionate defense of slavery before the war had made him one of the leading "Fire-Eaters" pushing secession and he had been one of Breckinridge's staunchest supporters in the 1860 election. Throughout the war, Miles had represented his state in the Confederate Congress. Unlike most of the other Fire-Eaters, he had remained an ally of Jefferson Davis, which Breckinridge supposed was the main reason he had been chosen as a delegate.

Miles produced a flask and, after taking a swig, offered it to Breckinridge, who quickly took a drink himself. The hot, fiery feeling of the whiskey as it flowed down his throat brought a smile to Breckinridge's face.

"I thought you'd like that," Miles said.

"I think I recognize it. Oscar Pepper bourbon, if I am not mistaken."

Miles' head drew back slightly. "I see the stories of your knowledge of bourbon are not exaggerated."

"I know the Pepper family. They make a very fine product."

"Did you bring along any bourbon?"

Breckinridge grinned. "I have two bottles in my own baggage. Gifts from Captain Weller, who served with me in the Orphan Brigade. His brother has a distillery in Kentucky that makes bourbon from wheat rather than rye."

"How interesting. Two bottles, you say?"

"That's right."

13

"I have one. I believe Postmaster Reagan has one. That makes four. Seems we shall have an enjoyable voyage to Canada."

"Let's hope so," Breckinridge replied. "It would have been a much faster trip had President Davis allowed us to pass through the United States."

"Yes, well, President Davis thought it best for us to avoid having to use Yankee trains to get to Toronto. He said it hinted that we were still dependent on them. Appearances are very important to him, you know."

"That's the truth, by God." He took another proffered swig of the flask. "How are our friends?"

"Postmaster Reagan is, I believe, being given a tour of the ship by Lieutenant Whittle." Miles chuckled. "Aleck is down in his cabin, fighting a losing battle with seasickness."

Breckinridge nodded, not surprised. Alexander Stephens, whom he knew well, had always been sickly. "Well, I hope the Vice President feels better this evening. The four of us need to sit down as soon as possible to hash out a proper strategy for the forthcoming talks with the Yankees."

Miles nodded. "It is a shame we did not get a chance to do so before departing Richmond. But we have all read President Davis's instructions."

"Of course. I've committed them to memory. But between you and me, William, the President is building castles in the sky. He really expects us to demand the cession of Missouri and Kentucky to the Confederacy? A referendum in Maryland? The return of freed slaves? We might make such demands if our armies occupied Washington and New York. As it is, we have not won the war. We have only avoided defeat, and that by a knife's edge. We are in no position to dictate terms."

"I hope you are mistaken," Miles said, a tone of caution creeping into his voice. "The slaves carried off by the Yankees during the war are the property of Confederate citizens. It only makes sense that they be returned. As for the border states, I would have thought that you, being a Kentucky man, would fight for their inclusion in the Confederacy."

"I would love nothing more than to see Kentucky become a part of the Confederacy. It would be the fulfillment of all my dreams. I fully intend to fight for a referendum in Kentucky at these negotiations. But we must face facts. What Davis wants us to ask for is completely unrealistic. Frankly, we'll be lucky if we regain Tennessee."

Breckinridge thought for a moment about the positions the opposing armies had occupied when the informal ceasefire had taken effect about six months before, not long after the presidential election in the North. In Virginia, Lee's army had held its ground outside Richmond and Petersburg, protected by a vast network of fortifications. In the Shenandoah Valley, Jubal Early's small but redoubtable force had held off the Union army of Phil Sheridan in an eventful campaign in which Breckinridge himself had played a crucial role.

In July, the Army of Tennessee had won its famous victory just north of Atlanta on the banks of Peachtree Creek. It had subsequently defeated a final Northern attempt to capture the city two months later. The beaten Union army under Ulysses Grant had withdrawn back towards Chattanooga when McClellan had taken office in March. In the distant lands west of the Mississippi River, Southern forces under John Bell Hood had regained much of Arkansas.

Despite the success of Confederate arms during 1864, the Union continued to occupy vast regions of the South. Virtually all of Tennessee, the Mississippi River Valley, northern Alabama, much of Northern Virginia, and large pockets of the Atlantic coast were under Yankee control. Breckinridge was smart enough to know that they would not give up those areas unless the Confederates offered concessions of their own. But what did they have with which to make concessions? Confederate forces occupied no Union territory aside from a few tiny bits of West Virginia and some of southwestern Missouri.

"Don't be so pessimistic, John," Miles said. "Remember that it was the North which sued for peace, not the South. The Northern people will not stand for a resumption of fighting. The Democratic majority in the House has already made it clear that it won't appropriate any more money for military action. Political reality dictates that the Yankees can't leave the conference without a peace treaty."

"We can't leave the conference without a peace treaty, either," Breckinridge countered. "Our economy is on the verge of collapse. Inflation is out of control. It will take years to repair our railroads. Frankly, we need peace more than the Yankees do. Without a peace treaty, there will be no investment from Europe or from the United States to help us rebuild our economy and resume normal trade."

"I don't disagree," Miles replied. "But unless the slaves carried off by the Yankees are returned to us, there will be no labor to work our fields. I'd go further than President Davis, in fact, for I believe we should insist that an agreement to return fugitive slaves to the Confederacy in the future be included in the peace treaty. Otherwise there will be no end to the number of slaves attempting to escape into the North."

Breckinridge looked at Miles carefully. The South Carolina congressman presented a friendly and affable countenance that contrasted sharply with most of his fellow Fire-Eaters. Yet Breckinridge knew that the man was a fanatical supporter of slavery and white supremacy. Before the war, he had even attempted to get legislation through Congress to legalize a resumption of the African slave trade.

"Trying to push the Yankees on slavery will be useless," Breckinridge said in a measured tone.

"Why?" Miles asked. "President McClellan hates the abolitionists."

"True, but the Republicans still control the Senate. Any treaty containing clauses calling for the return of escaped slaves will stand no chance of being ratified. We both know that. And any kind of new fugitive slave law will be rejected out of hand."

"We shall just have to persuade them, then," Miles said simply.

Breckinridge felt uneasy. If Miles took a strong stand on slavery, it would be much more difficult for the two sides to agree on a comprehensive peace treaty. Worse, it might fracture the unity of the Confederate delegation.

He decided to move the conversation on. "The border states and the status of the escaped slaves are only two of the issues confronting us. I expect the Yankees to demand that we assume a proportional share of the prewar national debt. They shall demand free navigation of the Mississippi River. Hell, they might even demand provisions in the treaty prohibiting us from seeking foreign alliances."

"That would infringe on our sovereignty," Miles said harshly. "If there's one thing the Yankees must agree to, it is

17

the complete and total political separation of the United States and Confederate States. The Yankees should have no more right to interfere in our internal affairs than the Emperor of China."

"The Yankees have already conceded that, just by agreeing to meet with us on a two-nation basis." As he said these words, Breckinridge recalled the intense, under-the-table negotiations that had taken place after McClellan had taken office. The newly-installed President had tried to interest Jefferson Davis in a convention of all the states to hammer out a peace agreement, but the Confederate leader had firmly rejected such an idea. Only negotiations on a two-nation basis had been acceptable. Under intense diplomatic pressure from Britain and France, who were eager for normal trade to resume, McClellan had given in.

"Border states. Runaway slaves. All these other issues." Miles took another swig from his flask. "I am glad you say you have more whiskey on hand, John. I have a strong suspicion we shall need a fairly large supply if we are to make it through the next few weeks."

*   *   *   *   *

He tried to focus on the pile of papers in his lap, but Breckinridge could not take his eyes off the Canadian countryside as it flew past outside his window. The train carrying them from Quebec to Toronto moved with a speed and smoothness he could scarcely believe. He had crisscrossed the Confederacy by rail many times, but Southern railroads were slow and rickety, worn down by years of poor maintenance and Yankee raids. The contrast between Confederate and British railroads was simply stunning.

18

Breckinridge knew that railroads in the United States were comparable to those of the British Empire. Industrial nations, after all, could devote the manpower, money, and material resources to maintaining outstanding transportation networks. Unless they found a way to free themselves, agricultural nations like the Confederacy would forever be dependent on others if they wanted such things as railroads. The same was true of ports, iron foundries, cotton mills, and just about everything else.

He thought for a moment of his friend Josiah Gorgas, the Chief of Ordnance in the Confederate War Department. The man had achieved logistical miracles, establishing factories and arsenals across the Confederacy that had provided for all the needs of the army in terms of weaponry. At no point during the war had the South lost a battle because it lacked sufficient rifles and ammunition.

If the South were going to prosper as a nation, it would need more men like Josiah Gorgas. It would need men who knew about railroads, who knew about shipping, who knew about manufacturing, and who knew about finance. Before the war, the South had relied on Northerners to do all these things. If the world were going to take the Confederacy's pretensions to nationhood seriously, that would have to change.

Breckinridge wondered if he himself would play a role in making this happen. He was a modest man, but was also aware that there was already speculation in the papers about what elected office he might seek when his tenure as Secretary of War was over. He had even been spoken of as a potential successor to Jefferson Davis.

He knew himself well enough to know that he was ambitious. Yet there was a difference between base ambition and the ambition which grew out of idealism. He never would have sought a single political office had he not genuinely intended to use his position to improve the lives of the people he represented. If he did run for Congress, or perhaps even the presidency itself, it would be because he wanted to put his natural talents and gifts at the service of the Southern people, to help them build the foundations of their new nation.

On the other hand, a large part of him wanted nothing so much as to retire from politics, resume his law practice, and devote the remainder of his life to his family. After a decade of political turmoil and four years of war, he was mentally and physically exhausted. There was no guarantee that his native state of Kentucky would even be a part of the Confederacy when the peace treaty was ratified. If Kentucky remained part of the Union, what would he do?

There was a soft knocking on the door.

"Come in," Breckinridge said.

The door slid open and revealed Vice President Alexander Stephens. He had a most peculiar appearance, as though some mysterious ailment had frozen his body when he had been a teenager yet allowed his face and skin to continue aging. Stephens himself often made self-effacing jokes about his appearance, describing himself as a "half-finished thing." It did not surprise Breckinridge that Stephens had never married. His eyes, Breckinridge thought, reflected an intense but hidden sadness.

However strange his outer shell, however, Stephens had one of the most powerful and incisive minds of any man Breckinridge had ever met. He had known Stephens well in pre-war Washington, where the Georgian had been one of the giants of the House of Representatives. He had sought compromise between North and South and fought secession until the last possible moment. During the war, he had avoided Richmond and devoted himself to improving conditions for Confederate troops and for Union captives held in prison camps. It was no secret that Stephens and Jefferson Davis detested one another, with Stephens having made several speeches denouncing the Confederate President for his policies on conscription, taxation, and the suspension of habeas corpus. Whatever else might be said about him, Alexander Stephens always stuck to his principles.

"I'm not disturbing you, John?" Stephens asked, his squeaky voice almost inaudible over the sounds of the train.

"Not at all, Aleck," Breckinridge responded. "Come in, please." He waved to the papers on his lap. "Just trying to get some work done."

"Aren't we all?" Stephens said as he shut the door and took a seat directly across from Breckinridge.

"What's on your mind?"

The Vice President looked at Breckinridge warily. "We may speak in confidence?"

"Of course." Any conversation begun with such words was bound to be interesting, Breckinridge thought.

Stephens nodded. "Judging from our conversations on board the *Shenandoah*, I don't think I'm wrong in assuming that you share my opinion about the instructions given to us by President Davis before leaving Richmond."

"That depends," Breckinridge said. "Is your opinion that his instructions are so unrealistic as to approach impossibility?"

"It is. I am glad to hear you say it so directly."

"Our commissions from the President compel us to present those terms to the Yankees at the beginning of the conference. They shall not agree to them, of course, and then the haggling will begin. It's an old story, Aleck. This is how treaties get made."

"One can only hope," Stephens replied. "But my fear is this. What if we present our terms as Davis has given them and the Yankees, rather than haggling, conclude that they cannot negotiate with us if our initial offer is so extreme. The conference could be over before it even has a chance to begin."

Breckinridge thought for a moment, shaking his head. "I said to Miles earlier that we need peace more than the Yankees do. And this is true. Nevertheless, the Northerners need peace, too. President McClellan's shaky hold on the government depends on this conference ending successfully. If the talks break down, he will be faced with the choice of either resuming the war, which would outrage the people and wouldn't get the support of the House, or allowing the status quo of a ceasefire without a genuine peace to continue indefinitely. Besides, with the Confederacy having gained recognition from Britain and France, McClellan knows he must have some sort of treaty. He can't allow the talks to break down."

"But neither can he allow us to walk away from these talks with everything we want. The Senate will not ratify any treaty that is seen as too favorable to us. If we begin the talks with Davis's draft of terms, we will be placing our Northern counterparts in an extremely delicate situation."

"I see," Breckinridge said thoughtfully. "And you think we should do what we can to give the Yankee commissioners an easier time of things, so as to give the conference a greater chance a success?"

"Quite so."

"You're proposing that we simply discard Davis's instructions?"

"I do not say we should discard them. I say that we should look upon them as advisory only."

"Now you're talking like a lawyer."

"We were both lawyers before we got into politics, John. In any event, since our goal in these talks must be the signing of a fair and honorable peace treaty, I feel we must give the Yankees enough slack to allow them to get some of what they want, as well. It will be difficult, even under the best circumstances, for them to get a treaty through the Senate. If we remain fixed on the terms Davis is insisting upon, it will be impossible."

Breckinridge sighed. "It's worse than that. Miles is intending to push the Yankees on issues relating to slavery. He not only wants a return of the slaves that Lincoln freed with the Emancipation Proclamation, but he wants to insist on a provision for the return of fugitive slaves in the future. A restoration of the old Fugitive Slave Act, in other words."

"The Yankees will never agree to either of those conditions," Stephens said.

"Miles apparently thinks he can persuade them. The man is charming, as half the ladies of Richmond can attest, but he has no chance whatsoever of convincing the Northern delegation on these particular points."

Stephens shrugged. "I believe in slavery no less than Miles. The subordination of the black race to the white race is rooted in nature. It is the great truth upon which our nation was founded. But I also recognize reality when I see it.

Pushing the Yankees on those issues might so inflame the Republican Party that they might try to push President McClellan into resuming the war. If enough Democrats sided with them, anything could happen."

"The British and the French are anxious for things to be regularized on this side of the Atlantic, so that proper trade can resume. They want our cotton and tobacco. And I don't think the Northern public would tolerate a resumption of hostilities, now that we have enjoyed several months of peace."

Breckinridge said this words matter-of-factly, without the emotion that he felt. Unlike Stephens, he had seen the war up close. He had ridden through the chaos, smoke, and thunder of battle. He had seen fields strewn with the corpses of what had been young men, like a sick harvest for the grim reaper. He had seen dysentery, typhoid, and other camp diseases carry off far more men than were killed in battle. He had personally written hundreds of letters to the parents, wives, and children of his fallen men, telling them that they were never going to see their loved ones again.

Since the unofficial ceasefire of November had become an official armistice with McClellan's inauguration in March, there had been none of this. There had been no more bloody battles. No endless casualty lists had been published in either the Northern or Southern newspapers. Many of the soldiers had returned home at the expiration of their enlistments. Like the early hints of a sunrise, peace was slowly beginning to dawn across the land.

Could the Northern people, having endured four years of war, seriously contemplate going to war again if the peace treaty their commissioners presented was not exactly what they wanted? Breckinridge couldn't believe it. By voting for McClellan and against Lincoln, the North had made a conscious decision that winning the war against the South was not worth the price in blood. Having now glimpsed the coming of peace, the Union would not willingly go back to war.

Stephens looked at him, as though reading his thoughts. "You and I have lived through interesting years, John. In 1860, did the Southern people really want to create a rebellion and plunge the country into a bloody war? Did the Northern people really want to wage such a war against the South? No, they did not. Events have a habit of carving their own paths through history, no matter what people might want. Assuming that the war cannot break out again is very dangerous, in my opinion."

"You might be right, Aleck," Breckinridge acknowledged.

"Then you agree with me that we cannot remain too closely wedded to Davis's instructions? That our primary goal must be to secure any kind of peace treaty, even if it is not the peace treaty we might want?"

"Yes, I do. But let us keep this between ourselves. Miles will be firm on slavery and Reagan will not like the idea of discarding Davis's instructions. We must test the waters before plunging in."

"That's the truth," Stephens said. "To be honest, I expect the waters to be awfully hot."

*   *   *   *   *

"How much longer, do you think?" Breckinridge asked. The train was passing structures that he assumed marked the outskirts of the city of Toronto.

"Twenty minutes, maybe?" replied John Reagan, Postmaster General of the Confederate States and the fourth member of the Southern peace delegation. "Lord knows I'll be happy to get off this train. After having been cooped up in either a ship or a railcar these last two weeks, I'm looking forward to stretching my legs."

Breckinridge chuckled slightly and nodded. Reagan's good cheer had made the journey to Toronto more agreeable than it otherwise would have been. A big man from the Texas frontier, Reagan reflected physical toughness more than mental acuity.

Although his acquaintance with Reagan had only begun when Breckinridge had joined the Cabinet a few months before, he had quickly come to respect him. Reagan might have looked like a Texas brawler, but he had proven to be an intelligent man with sharp political instincts, as well as a remarkably efficient administrator. Under his leadership, the Confederate postal service had actually made a profit.

In the discussions among the delegates during the trip, Reagan had been the most stalwart in asserting that their instructions from President Davis should be followed to the letter. Breckinridge assumed that Reagan's loyalty to Davis, along with his Trans-Mississippi constituency, was the primary reason he had been chosen as a delegate.

Breckinridge reflected on this for a moment. He himself had been chosen because of his prewar political prominence, his military record, and the fact that he was a border state man. Moreover, Breckinridge could naturally be expected to push strongly for the Yankees to give up Kentucky. Stephens, by contrast, had been chosen to placate those elements in the Confederate Congress who distrusted Davis, since the animosity between the Confederate President and Vice President was well known. Congressman Miles had

26

friends on both sides of the pro-Davis and anti-Davis divide, but had obviously been selected to represent the more outspoken pro-slavery elements from the Deep South.

Between the four of them, the states of Kentucky, Georgia, South Carolina and Texas were represented. Breckinridge had been somewhat surprised that a Virginian had not been selected, but there had been some grumbling in the newspapers that Virginia was overrepresented in the higher levels of the Confederacy. The commanders of the two principal Confederate armies, Robert E. Lee and Joseph Johnston, were both Virginians, as were a disproportionate number of major generals.

Breckinridge felt the train begin to decelerate. He turned to a young man sitting in the chair opposite.

"I think we'll be arriving soon, Mr. St. Martin. Is everything in order?"

"Completely, sir," St. Martin replied. "I spoke with the conductor an hour ago. The baggage master at the station has been instructed to give our party priority over other passengers."

Jules St. Martin, a young bureaucrat in the War Department, had accompanied the delegation as its secretary. Although Breckinridge found St. Martin competent enough, he assumed that the assignment would have gone to someone else were it not for the fact that the young man's much older brother-in-law was Secretary of State Judah Benjamin.

The station came into view a few minutes later. Staring out the window, Breckinridge was astounded to see a giant banner suspended from the overhang.

A large crowd had gathered on the platform. Breckinridge did not have a clue who any of them were, nor could he fathom why they were taking an interest in the arrival of the delegation. Toronto, he decided, must not be a particularly exciting town.

The next few minutes passed in a flurry of activity as the four Confederate delegates prepared to disembark from the train. Congressman Miles harangued St. Martin about ensuring the safety of his luggage. Vice President Stephens continually complained about the cool temperature, which Breckinridge himself found quite comfortable. Reagan simply appeared annoyed and anxious to get off the train as soon as possible.

Once St. Martin conveyed that the porters had their luggage in order, the Southerners stepped off the train and onto the platform. At that instant, a military fife and drum band began playing *Dixie*, the unofficial anthem of the Confederacy. A company of British infantry, wearing immaculate red uniforms, presented their arms in a salute to the delegates, their drill more precise than Breckinridge had ever seen from a Confederate unit. The crowd began cheering with genuine if not excessive enthusiasm.

"I wasn't expecting any of this," Stephens said. "Are we supposed to respond somehow?"

"I'm not sure," Breckinridge replied. "You're the head of the delegation. I think you are the one to respond."

"I have not the foggiest notion of what to do." Stephens' tone reflected an anxiety that didn't surprise Breckinridge, for his Georgia colleague had always been awkward in social situations.

Two men, one wearing a smart civilian suit and the other a pristine colonel's uniform, approached. The civilian was a portly man in his mid-sixties, his puffy cheeks covered with bushy sideburns. His appearance struck Breckinridge as mildly ridiculous. The colonel, however, looked altogether different. Tall and erect, with close-cropped hair and mustache, he carried himself with a sense of dignified disdain for those around him. His uniform jacket was covered in medals, among which Breckinridge recognized the emblem of the French Legion of Honor. His face was deeply scarred and there was something strange about his left eye, though Breckinridge couldn't place it.

"Gentlemen," the civilian said pleasantly. "Allow me to introduce myself. I am Francis Henry Medcalf, Mayor of Toronto. On behalf of Her Majesty Queen Victoria, I would like to welcome you to our fair city."

Stephens glanced nervously at Breckinridge for a moment and, after receiving a nod of encouragement, cautiously stepped forward and took Medcalf's extended hand. "I am Vice President Alexander Stephens." He paused uncertainly for a moment. "On behalf of the Confederate States of America, we thank you for your warm hospitality and willingness to host our peace talks with the United States."

"Peace should be the universal goal of all," Medcalf grandly replied.

Stephens introduced Breckinridge and the other two delegates to Medcalf, while St. Martin went off to see to the luggage. The colonel waited patiently, scarcely moving a muscle.

Medcalf took the colonel's elbow. "May I present Colonel Garnet Wolseley, of Her Majesty's Perthshire Light Infantry? Among other duties, he commands the militia in this part of Canada."

"I am honored to meet you gentlemen," Wolseley said, shaking each man's hand in turn. "I am especially glad to make your acquaintance, General Breckinridge. I have read about exploits during the war. Pray tell, is it true that you fielded cadets from the Virginia Military Institute at the Battle of New Market?"

Instantly, Breckinridge was back on the battlefield on that terrible and glorious day in May of 1864, just over a year earlier. He had been placed in command of Confederate forces in the Shenandoah Valley, charged with protecting the region's rich farmland. Leading a small force of about five thousand men, Breckinridge had been confronted with a larger Union army determined to seize control of the Valley. With Confederate forces hard pressed on other fronts by Grant and Sherman, the only reinforcements he had received had been the corps of cadets from VMI, numbering less than two hundred and fifty students. None of them had been older than eighteen. Breckinridge had prayed that he would not have to send the boys into the fighting.

The battle had been bloody and brutal. In the midst of a terrific thunderstorm, Breckinridge had aggressively attacked the larger Union force. At first all had gone well. The Union infantry had been driven back and Breckinridge had dispatched a force of cavalry to outflank the enemy and cut them off. But in the afternoon, his plan had begun to fall apart. A Union counter attack, coupled with fierce artillery barrage, had caused part of the Confederate line to collapse in confusion. He had been given no choice but to order the VMI cadets into the line to plug the gap, which they had unhesitatingly done.

30

The cadets had saved the day, securing the Southern line. A renewed Confederate assault had routed the Union army, driving it northwards in confusion and ensuring that the Shenandoah Valley remained in Confederate hands. The price had been high, with Breckinridge's small force losing more than five hundred men. Forty-seven of the cadets had been wounded; ten of the boys paid the ultimate price.

"It tore my heart in two to ask those boys to fight," Breckinridge said to Wolseley. "They fought like Spartans. I would have lost the battle without their help."

The two soldiers continued their own conversation while Breckinridge's three colleagues talked with Mayor Medcalf. "It is a glorious thing to die for one's country," Wolseley said. "To be given a chance to do so at such a young age was an honor for those young men. Those who survived will remember the battle as long as they live."

"I suppose so," Breckinridge replied, remembering the bodies of the slain VMI cadets. He forced his mind elsewhere, gesturing to the medals on Wolseley's chest. "You appear to be no stranger to battle yourself, sir."

Wolseley bowed his head respectfully. "Indeed not. I have had the honor to serve against Her Majesty's enemies on many battlefields around the world. It has all been glorious fun, I must say."

Breckinridge was taken aback. "I am not sure I would describe war as fun, sir."

Wolseley smiled, but not in a manner Breckinridge thought disrespectful. "I have heard the same response from many of you Americans. I visited the Confederacy in 1862, as I wanted to observe your war with the Northerners more directly. I met and spoke with your General Lee, who told me

31

that it was a good thing that war was so terrible, for otherwise we would grow too fond of it."

Breckinridge nodded. "He said something similar to me once, too."

Wolseley went on. "We British choose to see war in a different light than you Americans. What's wrong with being fond of war? Our forebears have given us a vast empire. We now gallivant around the world to protect and expand it. To us, you see, the world has been specially created for our own wild pleasures. War, with its sudden danger and maddening excitement, is surely the greatest pleasure of all. I know the unpleasant aspects of it all, of course. I'll limp the rest of my life on account of a Burmese bullet that I took in the leg. A Russian artillery shell in the Crimea mangled my body, ruined my face, and took the sight from my left eye. But war has earned me a certain amount of distinction and fame among my people. I hope to earn yet more."

Breckinridge knew a few Confederate soldiers who shared Wolseley's disdain of death and belief that war was something that could genuinely be enjoyed. His friend and fellow Kentuckian John Hunt Morgan certainly fit that category. It was a mystery to him how anyone could look over the ground after a battle, see the field covered with the mangled bodies of the dead, hear the groans and cries of the wounded, and feel that war was anything other than a horrifying nightmare.

Still, he admitted to himself that he liked Wolseley. Having never travelled outside of North America, Breckinridge had always enjoyed conversations with Britons and Europeans. "You are not a teetotaler, are you, Colonel Wolseley?"

"I am not," Wolseley responded with a smile. "I have considered becoming one, truth be told. I sometimes prohibit men under my command from drinking, depending on the state of their morale. In large social gatherings, I do not allow myself to drink, as I worry what I might say in a state of elevation."

"Would you be willing to join me for a whiskey sometime during my stay here in Toronto? I would enjoy exchanging our respective war stories."

Wolseley smiled. "That would be most agreeable. For that matter, I plan on making an excursion to Quebec sometime in the next few weeks to visit the battlefield on the Plains of Abraham. If your work at the peace conference does not interfere, you are more than welcome to join me."

"I would be honored to do so, Colonel, if it is at all possible," Breckinridge replied. He found the prospect of visiting one of the world's most famous battlefields exciting. "I expect the work of this conference to be difficult and time-consuming, but perhaps there will be occasions when we shall have to suspend the talks to obtain additional instructions from our respective governments."

"If you let me know in advance, I can schedule our excursion for one of those occasions."

"You are too kind," Breckinridge said. "I cannot ask you to go to such trouble on my account."

"It would be no trouble at all."

"Well, then, I shall send word to you when the time comes. In the meantime, if you wish to have that whiskey, my compatriots and I are staying at the Rossin House Hotel."

Wolseley smiled and extended his hand again. "You shall see me soon, General Breckinridge. It has been a true honor to meet you."

He shook Wolseley's hand, not knowing that he had made a friendship that would last the remainder of his life.

Chapter Two

The York County Court had thoughtfully vacated its building on Adelaide Street temporarily in order to give the two peace delegations a proper place in which to conduct their negotiations. It had been designed according to neo-Palladian architecture that reminded Breckinridge of the majestic public buildings he remembered from his days in Washington City, though the Canadian structure had a grayish austerity he found somewhat forbidding. He hoped it wasn't a portent of how the peace talks would go.

Escorted by a well-dressed Canadian valet, who had identified himself only as Edmund and been put at their service by the Canadian authorities, the Confederate delegation entered the central hall where the talks were to take place. Breckinridge saw an immense oak table, perhaps fifteen feet long and five feet wide. It seemed far too large for the eight delegates and their two secretaries.

"Your breakfast has been prepared, gentlemen," Edmund said, waving his hand over the table.

It looked sumptuous. The smell of ham, fried tomatoes and mushrooms, rolls just out of the oven, and black pudding almost overwhelmed Breckinridge's senses. Trays of freshly brewed coffee lay on both sides of the table. A hand bell was placed in the middle of the table, amongst the food.

"Please ring the bell if you need anything," Edmund said. "If you'll excuse me, I will return to the lobby and wait for your counterparts." He bowed his head slightly and went out the way they had come in.

Congressman Miles happily took a seat and began to eat. "And then to breakfast, with what appetite you have," he said pleasantly. Breckinridge recognized the quote was Shakespeare's, though he could not recall from which play the line had come.

"Shouldn't we wait for the Northern delegation to arrive?" Reagan asked. "Don't want to be rude."

"Why?" Miles responded. "It's eight o'clock, which was the agreed upon time. If the Yankees are late, it's not our fault."

"Perhaps, but it wouldn't hurt to be polite," Breckinridge said. "We're likely to be spending quite a bit of time with these gentlemen over the next few weeks."

"Weeks?" Miles asked with a grin. "I wonder if you're being too pessimistic. If all goes well, we could have these negotiations wrapped up within five or six days."

"Or if our Northern friends decide to be stubborn, we could be celebrating Christmas here in Toronto," Reagan noted sourly.

Miles finished chewing a mouthful of ham and swallowed. "Well, the sooner we conclude our business and return home, the better. The prospect of spending winter in Canada is not pleasant, to say the least."

Breckinridge poured himself a cup of coffee, added cream, and took a grateful sip. For just a moment, he recalled the improvised coffee he had been forced to consume while serving in the Confederate army, on account of the Union blockade. It had been made of ground peanuts or chicory root and had tasted positively awful. He knew he would never take the simple pleasure of a decent cup of coffee for granted again.

At that moment, Edmund returned to the room and looked at the Confederates with just a hint of uncertainty.

"The Union delegation has arrived, gentlemen."

Five men entered the room behind Edmund, three wearing stylish civilian suits of dark cloth, one wearing a rather less impressive suit, and one wearing the blue uniform of a Union major general. They halted upon seeing the Confederates, almost as though they sensed danger. Miles stood from his chair. For an awkward moment, they men stared at one another across the room, neither side knowing precisely what to say.

The magnitude of the moment struck Breckinridge. The peace conference between the Union and the Confederacy, which would hopefully bring to an end a war that had killed more than half a million people, was about to begin.

Edmund broke the silence with the most mundane of statements. "As you can see, gentlemen, breakfast has been prepared. I already told the Southern gentlemen that you may ring the bell if you have a need for anything else. Otherwise, no one shall disturb you."

One of the men in civilian clothes, Secretary of State Horatio Seymour, turned to Edmund. "Thank you, young man. You may retire." The valet again bowed his head and withdrew from the room.

A smiling Miles strode forward with an outstretched hand. "Good morning, Mr. Secretary," he said pleasantly, shaking Seymour's hand. "And Vice President Hamlin! It is good to see you! Mr. Black, how are you today? And I assume you are General Porter? I am pleased to meet you!"

The ten men exchanged greetings and handshakes for a few minutes. Breckinridge was well acquainted with Secretary of State Seymour, Attorney General Jeremiah Black and former Vice President Hannibal Hamlin, having met them on many occasions in Washington City before the war. General Fitz John Porter was unknown to him, though Breckinridge was impressed by the firmness of his handshake. He also did not know the fifth man, assuming him to be the delegation's secretary.

"Shall we enjoy breakfast before commencing our business, gentlemen?" Breckinridge asked.

"I do not see why not," Seymour replied amiably.

As the ten men took their seats and began to eat, Breckinridge looked across the table at the four Union commissioners. Secretary of State Horatio Seymour had a prominent forehead and a mass of disheveled hair that seemed to be growing out from the back of his head. His smile was warm but seemed to conceal much more than it revealed. He had been the Governor of New York during the war, supporting the war effort while bitterly denouncing conscription, censorship and the Emancipation Proclamation. Joining the ranks of the Copperheads after the Confederate victory at Atlanta in the summer of 1864, he had been made

Secretary of State by McClellan immediately after the latter's inauguration. Rumor said that he was the true decision-maker in the McClellan administration.

The inaptly named Hannibal Hamlin had a soft and passive appearance, with a large nose, bushy eyebrows, and somewhat sunken eyes. To Breckinridge, he looked more like a professor than a politician. He also knew that Hamlin was an intelligent man of strong convictions. Before the war, Hamlin had been a firm opponent of the extension of slavery into the territories, though he had never been a radical abolitionist like Charles Sumner or Thaddeus Stevens. While serving as Lincoln's Vice President during the war, he had not played an active role and had held little influence. Having held the same office himself, Breckinridge could empathize.

When he had heard that the former Vice President was one of the Union delegates, Breckinridge had been surprised. He had discussed the question with his fellow delegates during their journey to Toronto. They had finally concluded that Hamlin had been selected as a gesture of goodwill to the Republicans, who still held a diminished majority in the Senate and would need to ratify any treaty that came out of the talks. What role Hamlin would play in the talks remained to be seen.

Breckinridge knew the third commissioner, Jeremiah Black, quite well. A Pennsylvanian, he had become one of the best known lawyers in the country during the 1840s. When Breckinridge had been Vice President, Black had served in the Cabinet under Buchanan as Attorney General. He had not played a major role during the war, however, and had only been saved from obscurity when McClellan returned him to his old post as Attorney General. Breckinridge thought that his presence at the conference, like his appointment to the Cabinet, was probably intended to solidify support in the politically crucial Keystone State.

General Fitz John Porter struck Breckinridge as having an appropriately martial appearance and his uniform was impeccable. From what Breckinridge had read, he was a New Hampshire man who had gone against the traditions of his navy family by joining the army. He had fought as a division and corps commander in the Eastern Theater for the first half of the war. Southern generals in Lee's army, usually disdainful of their Yankee enemies, held Porter in high regard and considered him an unusually crafty and dangerous opponent.

Porter's rising star had fallen disastrously in the winter of 1862-63. A close associate of George McClellan, Porter had been essentially purged from the army by Lincoln's Secretary of War, Edwin Stanton, following McClellan's removal from army command. Court-martialed on trumped-up charges of disobeying orders during the Second Battle of Manassas, and convicted by a military tribunal stacked with Stanton's lackeys, Porter had been dismissed from the army under a cloud of ignominy. One of McClellan's first acts upon being inaugurated as President had been to pardon Porter, restore him to the army and appoint him as one of the commissioners to the peace conference.

The fifth Union man was Seth Williams, the secretary to the Union delegation. In a very brief conversation, Breckinridge learned that he had been a staff officer in the Army of the Potomac during the war. He seemed anxious to remain quiet, so Breckinridge troubled him no further.

The men talked amiably across the table as they ate their breakfast. Inquiries were made about old friends not seen since before the war. In response to a question from Stephens, Hamlin described the new dome over the United States Capitol. There was a brief and pleasant discussion about which plays were being shown in the theaters of Washington City and Richmond.

After forty five minutes, the bell was rung so that the used plates and assorted refuse of breakfast could be taken away. Edmund's staff brought additional trays of coffee and then again withdrew from the room. The men rearranged their seating, with the four men from each delegation sitting directly across from one another and the two respective secretaries sitting at each end of the table, writing materials close at hand.

Seymour cleared his throat. "Well, gentlemen, shall we begin our business?"

"The sooner the better," Miles replied. Breckinridge looked at him askance. It would have been more fitting had Stephens, the acknowledged head of the delegation, to have responded to Seymour's words.

"Very well, then," Seymour said. "I believe we should commence these negotiations with an agreement among all ten of us, delegates and secretaries alike, to keep our deliberations strictly confidential."

"Agreed," Stephens said quickly. "The members of the Constitutional Convention in 1787 were wise enough to agree to a similar protocol. Had they not done so, they could not have negotiated as freely as they did for fear of a public backlash before their work was completed."

"If it was good enough for the Founding Fathers, it should be good enough for us, don't you think?" Seymour said.

"Indeed," Stephens replied.

"I see no need to put this in writing. All at this table are gentlemen. Are we agreed?" Seymour glanced at every man at the table, receiving nods of assent from everyone. He then glanced at a grandfather clock against one of the walls.

"It is quarter past nine. Why do we not lay out our initial terms before breaking for lunch at noon?"

"That would be agreeable to us," Stephens said. "May I start?"

"By all means."

"The first and most important clause of the treaty, which we must insist upon before any further discussions are held, is that the United States acknowledges the full and complete independence of the Confederate States."

Stephens spoke these words so matter-of-factly, as though his squeaky voice were describing the weather, that it caught Breckinridge off guard. It seemed absurd that something of such momentous import could be summed up in a single sentence. Across the table, Hamlin and Porter looked pained, as though reminded of the recent death of a loved one, though Black had no reaction at all. Seymour slowly nodded and responded.

"We would not be sitting down at this table with you if we had not already agreed to this, Mr. Stephens. I own that neither I nor any other Northern man is happy about it. I would have given a great deal to have maintained the Union. Nevertheless, facts are facts. The United States has failed to defeat the Confederacy, you have secured the diplomatic recognition of the great powers in Europe, and acknowledging your independence is simply a concession to reality."

"We are glad to hear you say it," Miles replied. "Had you acknowledged our independence when we chose to leave the Union in 1861, hundreds of thousands of lives might have been spared."

To the surprise of Breckinridge, Hamlin replied. "And had you not broken the sacred ties that bound the Union together out of a desire to maintain the detestable institution of slavery, not only might those lives have been spared but the great republic created by the Founding Fathers could have been saved as well."

"I resent those words, Mr. Hamlin," Stephens said sharply. "I strove as hard as a man can strive to hold the Union together. I opposed secession until the last possible moment. It was only when it became clear that the North was absolutely determined to deprive the South of its most cherished rights that I sadly turned my back on the Union."

"What rights?" Hamlin asked. "The right to exploit the labor of other human beings?"

Miles replied, speaking in a patronizing tone. "We believe that our peculiar institution forms the best framework for the proper relations between the white and black races. We believe slavery is ordained by God. By defending slavery, we are but doing God's will. I myself look upon the victory of the Confederacy as a vindication for the Southern way of life and a sign that our cause has the favor of the Almighty."

"I frankly doubt the slaves see it that way," Hamlin replied grimly. "And I don't recall Jesus Christ saying anything kind about slavery in the Gospels."

"Let us not become distracted," Stephens interjected. "Am I to understand that the United States concedes to the acknowledgement of full Confederate independence?"

Seymour nodded. "We do. Reluctantly, I must say, but we do."

"Will there be any objection to having that fact stated in a specific article of the treaty, so there is no possible misunderstanding?"

Seymour shrugged. "I suppose not."

"That is very good," Stephens said. He glanced over at Breckinridge, a rare smile on his face. None of this had been unexpected, but it still represented the culmination of years of struggle.

General Porter now cleared his throat. "If you gentlemen will forgive me, I would like to discuss those articles pertaining to purely military matters. I do hope that we can settle these questions quickly and amicably."

Stephens and Miles both looked at Breckinridge. As Secretary of War and the only Confederate commissioner who had served in uniform, it was natural for him to take the lead on such questions.

"Go ahead, General Porter," Breckinridge said.

"Obviously, the treaty will say that the state of war between the two nations has come to an end."

"Of course."

"To get into the details, I propose that, upon the date of ratification, the United States will begin a withdrawal of its forces from the territory of the Confederacy that it currently occupies, to be completed in three months."

"Why three months?" Miles asked. "Can it not be done more quickly?"

"It is a complicated logistical undertaking to move so many thousands of men, Congressman," Porter replied. "Railroads and river steamers must be prepared, roads cleared for large units of marching men, supply depots organized along the route, that sort of thing."

"General Porter is correct," Breckinridge said. "Three months seems to be a proper amount of time."

"The treaty must also include a provision for Confederate troops to withdraw from any Union territory they happen to occupy," Hamlin said quickly. "If I am not mistaken, rebel troops occupy small parts of southwestern Missouri, eastern Tennessee, and southern West Virginia. I don't want to see them still sitting there when the treaty goes into effect."

"Missouri, Tennessee, and West Virginia are Confederate territory," Miles replied instantly.

Breckinridge raised his hand to quiet his fellow delegate. "We have not yet begun discussion on the question of borders. Let us handle the technical aspects of this question first."

Miles shrugged. "Very well. We shall come to the issue soon enough, I suppose."

"No doubt," Seymour said from across the table. He looked at Breckinridge. "Are we agreed that the treaty contain provisions for a Confederate withdrawal from all Union territory as well?"

"Of course," Breckinridge said. "While we remain on the subject of military matters, the treaty must also stipulate the end of the United States naval blockade." The blockade had not been strongly enforced since the official armistice had gone into effect three months earlier, but it was technically still in effect. The resumption of Southern trade depended on its termination.

"If the treaty says that the war has come to an end, doesn't that necessarily require the end of the naval blockade?" Hamlin asked.

"Legally, I believe that is correct," Seymour replied. "A blockade is an act of war, so the establishment of peace automatically will mean an end to the blockade."

"Perhaps so," Breckinridge said. "We would still like it enshrined in the text of the treaty."

Seymour shrugged. "I have no objection, so long as the same clause requires your commerce raiders to cease their attacks on our ships and return to port. Is that agreeable?"

"Completely." Breckinridge knew that the two surviving Southern cruisers had already ended their depredations on Union merchant shipping. Including such a provision cost the Confederacy nothing and allowed the Union to save face.

"Which brings us to the exchange of prisoners," Porter said.

Breckinridge took a deep breath. When the armistice had gone into effect, both sides still held tens of thousands of prisoners, most of them contained in makeshift and unsanitary camps. Andersonville, the largest Confederate prison camp, was a nightmarish place where thousands of Northern prisoners had died from disease and exposure. Prison camps in the North, despite its vastly superior resources, were little better. Countless Southern captives had perished in places like Point Lookout in Maryland and Elmira Prison in New York.

It was a personal issue for Breckinridge. His own son Cabell had spent months in a Union prison camp after being taken prisoner at Missionary Ridge. Moreover, hundreds of men from the Orphan Brigade had been captured during the fighting around Atlanta. Breckinridge felt duty-bound to help them.

Although prisoner exchanges had resumed when the fighting had come to an end, they were not proceeding very well. The Confederates had refused to abandon their policy of treating captured black troops as escaped slaves rather than as regular prisoners-of-war, causing abolitionists to demand a halt to the exchanges. Threatened Union retaliation had prevented the Confederate authorities from actually returning the black prisoners to the plantations, leaving thousands of captives on both sides confined to the prison camps in a state of legal limbo.

Congressman Miles, to Breckinridge's disappointment, spoke first. "We have absolutely no objection to a complete release of all legitimate prisoners once peace is established."

"What do you mean by 'legitimate'?" Seymour asked.

"I think he's referring to white prisoners," Hamlin said sourly.

"I am," Miles replied without compunction. "Under Confederate law, the black prisoners are escaped slaves and must be returned to their owners. After all, it only makes sense that the horses and other draft animals appropriated by one side from the other be returned, so why not the slaves as well?"

Seymour, Black and Porter all frowned, but Hamlin's eyes grew angry. Breckinridge glanced sideways at Miles, wordlessly trying to tell him to be quiet. There was nothing to be gained by such talk, which was obviously intended solely to needle the Northern negotiators. Breckinridge could not understand why Miles did not see this.

"It is our position that every soldier of the United States Army is a legitimate prisoner-of-war, no matter what his color or race," Hamlin stated firmly.

47

"And our position is that those slaves are the property of Southern citizens and should be returned to their owners," Miles replied. His smug countenance made it clear that he considered the opinion of the Northerners to be of no concern.

"Hell will freeze over before we allow those brave men to be returned to a state of slavery," Hamlin said.

"Moreover, not all of them are escaped slaves," Black pointed out. "Many of them are free men from the North who have never been slaves at all. Even if we accepted your legal position, which we do not, those men would have to be released along with the white prisoners."

Miles shrugged. "If it's impossible to differentiate between the two, it's safe to assume that the blacks in question are slaves merely pretending to be free men. They're very clever about that sort of thing, you know. If their owners cannot be identified, they should be sold by the Confederate government at auction."

"Never," Hamlin said coldly. He sat back in his chair and folded his arms across his chest.

For his part, Breckinridge believed that the Northern position was correct, though he obviously couldn't say so. The freed slaves who had enlisted in the Union Army could never be returned to a state of slavery. If the treaty contained such a provision, the Republican-controlled Senate would never ratify it and the two delegations were wasting their time.

Besides, as far as Breckinridge was concerned, only a delusional plantation owner would want those slaves returned. Having tasted freedom and the sense of dignity that came with military training and discipline, none of those men could be compelled to return to the abject life of a field slave. Trying to force them back into servitude would cause a series of slave revolts across the Confederacy, making the nightmare of many Southerners into a terrifying reality.

Miles was still talking. "And it's not just the soldiers, of course. Under Lincoln's so-called Emancipation Proclamation, a blatantly unconstitutional act, large numbers of slaves were stolen from their owners and taken away. We require that those slaves be returned to their owners."

"That's outrageous!" Hamlin shouted.

"I must agree," Seymour said more calmly. "I was not a friend to the Emancipation Proclamation when President Lincoln issued it, but what you are asking is simply not possible. Even if we wanted to do it, logistical reality precludes it. The slaves freed under the Proclamation number in the hundreds of thousands, I should think. It's impossible to even know where they all are."

"It is my understanding that almost all of them fled from the occupied area of the South into the Union proper once the armistice took effect," Black said. "With the coming of peace, they fear being enslaved once again."

"A fear that is sadly justified, apparently," Hamlin said through gritted teeth.

"I understand the difficulties involved," Miles replied. "But you cannot ignore the property rights of thousands of Southerners simply because doing otherwise is problematic."

"There was nothing unconstitutional or illegitimate about the manner in which those slaves were liberated," Hamlin said sternly. "They are now free men and women. There's nothing you can do about that."

"We can refuse to sign the peace treaty," Miles replied with measured calmness.

Breckinridge and Stephens exchanged knowing and worried glances with one another. Miles was acting foolishly. In their pre-conference discussions, Stephens and Breckinridge had suggested waiting to hear what the Yankees would say regarding the slaves freed by the Emancipation Proclamation. Miles had proposed demanding a return of the freed slaves and Reagan, stressing the need to follow Davis's instructions, had sided with Miles. Breckinridge now dearly wished that they had resolved that deadlock before the conference had begun. Miles, it seemed, had no compunction about seizing the issue and running with it, despite what he and Stephens thought.

Miles was still talking. "One more thing. In addition to you dropping claims regarding the slave soldiers being held in Southern prison camps and returning those slaves illegally taken by your troops, we require the treaty to include a clause that will reestablish the Fugitive Slave Act. Once our two nations are at peace with one another, we cannot have our slaves constantly running off into Northern territory."

"Surely you are not serious," Seymour said.

"I'm beginning to question your sanity, Congressman," Hamlin observed.

"There is no need for insults, Mr. Vice President," Miles replied, taking a sip from his cup of coffee.

Seymour spoke next. "Your demand regarding the prisoners is highly questionable and your call for the return of freed slaves even more so. But requiring the United States to enact a Fugitive Slave Law is far beyond the bounds of the ridiculous. You cannot expect us to entertain such an idea even for a moment."

"We not only expect it, Mr. Secretary. We require it."

"We might as well get up and leave these talks now," Hamlin said, turning to his fellow Northerners.

Breckinridge felt a growing sense of panic. His worst fears were coming to pass right before his eyes. Miles was remaining steadfast on the slavery questions and neither Breckinridge nor Stephens could intervene without making it appear that the Confederate delegation was fracturing from within. He had to pour water on the fire before it became too hot.

"Perhaps we should move on and come back to these issues later," Breckinridge said.

"I'm happy to move on to the next subject, but I think it's clear that slavery is going to be the biggest stumbling block to our work here," Seymour said. "I wish Congressman Miles would be more reasonable on the subject."

Miles's only response was to chuckle slightly.

"Perhaps we should begin discussions about borders," Porter suggested.

"That's likely to be as acrimonious as slavery," Stephens said sourly. "But we must get to it, I suppose. Shall we present our terms first or would you like the honor?"

Seymour gestured politely with his hands. "Feel free, Mr. Stephens."

"Very well," the Confederate Vice President responded. "We require that the United States recognize Confederate authority in Tennessee, Kentucky, Missouri and the New Mexico Territory. We also require that the territory of so-called West Virginia be returned to the State of Virginia proper and that the illegitimate state government be disavowed by the United States. Finally, we require that the people of Maryland to be given the option of joining the Confederacy via a plebiscite of the voting population."

"Oh, you require us to do these things, do you?" Seymour said sarcastically. "Well, here are our requirements. We require the Confederacy to abandon any and all legal claim to West Virginia, Kentucky, Tennessee, Missouri, and the New Mexico Territory. As for a plebiscite in Maryland, you can forget that idea. You cannot expect us to allow Washington City, our capital, to be surrounded by Confederate territory. Furthermore, we require that the State of Louisiana, much of which is occupied by our forces, be given the opportunity for a plebiscite to decide whether it shall be part of the Union or the Confederacy."

"Madness," Miles said. "Utter madness. Do you really expect us to accept such terms?"

"I don't see why our terms are any more unreasonable than yours," Black observed.

"I acknowledge that the status of Kentucky and Missouri is somewhat confused, what with two competing state governments for both states," Miles said. "But the secession of Tennessee has never legally been in doubt. It was approved by a vote of the people in 1861. Tennessee is unquestionably a Confederate state. This so-called West Virginia is a legal fiction, as the land in question clearly belongs to the State of Virginia. And a plebiscite in Louisiana would be an absurd waste of time, since everyone knows the people strongly favor the Confederacy."

"If they strongly favor the Confederacy, why would you fear a plebiscite?" Black asked.

"I don't fear one. I just think one would be a waste of time and money."

52

While Miles and Black argued, Breckinridge thought over the proposed Union terms. As he had feared, the Yankees had refused even to consider the possibility of Kentucky joining the Confederacy. He sensed that no amount of adroit negotiating was going to change this and his heart was filled with sadness. For him, it meant that the rest of his life would be spent in exile from his home, separated from his friends and condemned to return to the scenes of his youth only as a visiting foreigner.

For just a moment, Breckinridge's mind went back to October 17, 1862, one of the bleakest days of his life. After fighting at Shiloh and Baton Rouge, Breckinridge and his men had been called north to reinforce Braxton Bragg's invasion of Kentucky. It was hoped that Breckinridge, so popular with the men of the Bluegrass State, might encourage his fellow Kentuckians to throw off the Yankee yoke and enlist in the Confederate Army. Alternately marching along dusty roads or riding in cramped rail cars, Breckinridge had brought his division, including his beloved Orphan Brigade, to Knoxville in eastern Tennessee.

They had begun the march north on October 15. The blue skies had been beautiful, the autumn air crisp and fresh, the trees covering the Great Smoky Mountains a splendid combination of red, yellow, and green. His spirits, and those of the Orphans, had been high. The men had marched jauntily, singing songs, cheering and waving their hats whenever Breckinridge had ridden past their columns. He and his Orphans had awoken on the morning of October 17 knowing that a solid day's march would bring them across the border and back into their beloved Kentucky. Breckinridge had felt like Odysseus returning to the island of Ithaca.

That dream had died when a dispatch arrived from Bragg ordering the column to turn around and march back to Knoxville. Despite winning a victory at Perryville, Bragg had inexplicably decided to abandon Kentucky and retreat back to Tennessee. With broken hearts and downcast eyes, Breckinridge and his Orphans had turned and marched south, away from the Kentucky border. In the years since, Breckinridge still had yet to return to the land of his birth.

He shook his head, as if trying to rid himself of the memory. He had to set aside his personal feelings and concentrate on the matter at hand. He thought again of the Union proposals. Their demand that a plebiscite be held in Louisiana was obviously a negotiating ploy, since most of the state outside of New Orleans remained in Southern hands and any such vote would surely result in a Confederate landslide. Breckinridge was certain that the Union men intended to drop this particular demand later on, in exchange for a Confederate concession on something else. He filed this thought away for future reference.

The truly surprising Yankee demand was that the South drop its claim to Tennessee altogether. He hadn't expected the Yankees to unilaterally recognize Confederate authority in the state, but he had expected them to at least offer a plebiscite. It was true that Tennessee had a functioning state government loyal to the United States, led by former Senator Andrew Johnson, and that the people living in the eastern part of the state were generally loyal to the Union. Taken as a whole, though, Tennessee was a thoroughly Confederate state. Far more Tennesseans served in the Confederate Army than in the Union Army.

Breckinridge considered the possibility that the Northern position on Tennessee was, like the idea of a plebiscite in Louisiana, a negotiating ploy designed to pressure the South to abandon its claims to the other states and territories. Yet the fact remained that the Union Army occupied almost the entire state, with only a few bits of eastern Tennessee under Confederate control.

These thoughts were swept aside when General Porter cleared his throat to speak.

"There is one other consideration regarding borders," he said. "We require that the territory of Virginia between the Potomac River and the Rappahannock River be ceded to the United States."

"Why?" Breckinridge asked. The land in question represented a considerable chunk of Virginia.

"Washington City is the capital of the United States. If Confederate territory were to extend up to the Potomac River, the capital would be under constant military threat."

"That's your problem, not ours," Miles retorted. "It's not our fault that the Potomac flows where it does."

"Would you consent to have a couple of hundred Union artillery pieces within range of the Capitol Building in Richmond after the peace treaty is signed?" Seymour asked. "If so, perhaps we could include such a clause in the final draft of the treaty."

Miles ignored the quip. "We shall not consent to let the good people of Northern Virginia live under the Yankee yoke. Of that you can be sure!" To emphasize his point, the South Carolinian slammed his fist down onto the table.

Coffee cups rattled and the fuller ones spilled out onto the saucers. On either end of the table, St. Martin and Williams held down their inkpots to prevent any spillage onto the notes they were taking. A sudden silence descended on the room. Breckinridge could sense the heightened tension between the eight men. As he had expected, on the issues of slavery and final borders, nerves were already stretched to the breaking point. Worse still, the negotiations had only just begun.

Reagan chuckled, breaking the silence. "I am glad that we are approaching the time we agreed to break for lunch. I don't think I'm wrong when I say that we could all use some time to cool our passions."

"Well, as least we can all agree on that," Hamlin replied.

"Very well, then," Stephens said. "Shall we reconvene here in two hours?"

Seymour glanced at his colleagues and saw no disagreement. "Fine by us."

*   *   *   *   *

Each member of the Confederate delegation had been allocated a separate room in the Rossin House Hotel, arguably the finest such establishment in Toronto. In addition, the delegation had been given a separate suite to be used as a space for private meetings and communal meals. In that room, Breckinridge picked at his lunch of roast beef and potatoes while listening to Congressman Miles go on and on about the Northerners.

"Silly people, these Yankees," Miles mused. "They simply do not understand our ways. How can they fail to see that our peculiar institution is the best possible relationship between the white and black races? I wonder if it's even worth talking with them sometimes. It's just like before the war."

"It does no good to speak of the Northerners as though they were Southerners," Stephens replied. "Like it or not, they do not understand our peculiar institution. We cannot change their minds about it. We have to talk to them on their own terms."

"Yes, well, it's no wonder they can't even run their own country."

Breckinridge set his knife and fork down. "Your proposals regarding slavery are not worth discussing at the present time. We should concentrate on the question of the disputed states, where negotiation may at least lead to something positive."

"The Yankees seem as intransigent on the question of borders as they do on slavery," Miles observed.

"Perhaps, but some movement is possible. Regarding Tennessee, Kentucky, and Louisiana, I believe that the terms laid out by our Northern counterparts are, on the face of it, unacceptable. They, in turn, see our terms as unacceptable. Now that both sides have the other side's initial terms, the haggling is sure to begin."

"That's true, by God," Reagan said. "This is going to be a long process, I fear."

"Before we talk about borders, let me ask if there are any other outstanding issues we wish to lay on the table when the talks resume," Stephens said.

Reagan answered. "According to the instructions from the President, we are to demand financial compensation for the damage done to Southern property by Union armies during the war."

"They won't give a penny," Breckinridge predicted. "If anything, I expect them to counter with a demand that the Confederacy assume a portion of the prewar United States debt. That's what I'd do in their place, anyway."

"Thus leaving that part of the talks in a stalemate," Stephens observed.

"Perhaps so," Reagan said. "But that is what we are instructed to ask for by the President. We should not deviate from his instructions, at least not without very good cause."

"We'll see what the Yankees say about that when it comes up," Breckinridge replied. "Now, what was your opinion of the talks about borders?"

Miles snorted in contempt. "I did not like the way they dismissed our rightful claims to Tennessee so glibly. They did not even offer the option of a plebiscite for the state. Apparently they expect us to hand it over to them on a silver platter."

"The tens of thousands of Tennessee men currently in the Confederate Army might object to that, I suspect," Stephens said.

"Quite so, but the fact is that almost the entire state is occupied by Union forces," Breckinridge said. "We cannot expect the Yankees to agree to a plebiscite unless they receive concessions from us on other issues."

"And where can we offer concessions?" Miles asked.

Breckinridge thought for a moment. "Perhaps we might show a willingness to abandon our demand for a plebiscite in Maryland if they agree to allow one in Tennessee. The United States will never agree to it anyway, so by abandoning it we might make them more willing to compromise elsewhere."

"What about Kentucky?" Reagan asked. "Are you saying you want to give up on Kentucky as well as Maryland?"

"No," Breckinridge said sharply. "No. Kentucky is too important. We must fight for it." As he spoke these words, Breckinridge asked himself if he were speaking as an unbiased public servant or as a man pursuing his own personal agenda. He did not like the thought.

Stephens spoke next. "Might it be wise to agree to the Union demand for a plebiscite in Louisiana? They expect us to fight them on that point, but I see no reason to do so. I expect the state would vote heavily in favor of remaining a part of the Confederacy."

"Only if the Yankees allow the elections to be fair," Miles replied. "With New Orleans occupied by the Union Army, how can we trust the results of any such election?"

"We can insist on provisions being put in place to ensure a fair election without conceding other points. In any case, our price for agreeing to the Louisiana plebiscite could be having a similar election in Tennessee."

For a moment, Breckinridge found himself wondering what the Secretary of State, Judah Benjamin, would have thought of Stephens's proposal to allow a plebiscite in Louisiana. Benjamin was a Louisiana man who made his home in New Orleans. Had it not been for the fact that he was presently in Europe, shuttling between Paris and London trying to secure loans for the Confederacy, he almost certainly would have been a member of the peace commission. Breckinridge found himself wishing that the oft-discussed transatlantic telegraph had been completed, as it would have been useful to get Benjamin's opinion on the matter.

"And if the Yankees counter with a demand that we abandon the plebiscite in Maryland as well?" Reagan asked.

"I'd agree to it," Breckinridge said quickly. "I never expected the Yankees to agree to the Maryland plebiscite anyway, nor do I think the vote would be in our favor even if one were to be held. Tennessee and Kentucky are the prizes we must fight for. Agreeing to a plebiscite in Louisiana, which we will win, and abandoning a plebiscite in Maryland, which we would lose, seem more than worth it if we can have referendums in Tennessee and Kentucky. Tennessee we would certainly win, and likely Kentucky as well."

"And if the Yankees offer a plebiscite in Tennessee but not Kentucky?" Miles said, looking Breckinridge squarely in the eye. "What then?"

Breckinridge thought for a moment before replying. "Kentucky is dear to my heart, as you all well know. The idea of living out the rest of my life in exile from my home, separated from all that I hold dear, causes me much pain. But my task here is to fulfill my oath to the Confederacy, not to serve my own personal ends. If I look facts in the face, it's obvious that we have a chance of reclaiming Tennessee in these talks, while claiming Kentucky is not nearly as likely. Still, we must fight for the Bluegrass State."

"I frankly doubt that the Northerners will agree to referendums in both Tennessee and Kentucky," Stephens said.

Miles chuckled. "Looks like you may have to run for office from another state, John."

"That's the least of my concerns," Breckinridge replied.

While the others continued discussing Tennessee and Kentucky for the next few minutes, Breckinridge found himself distracted by the quip Miles had made. After all, what did the future hold for him? He was only in his mid-forties and had already earned more political and military glory than all but a handful of men earned in their entire lives. Might it be best to retire from politics when his time as Secretary of War was over? The prospect of a thriving private law practice and time to spend with his children, as well as the possibility of finally traveling to Europe, was certainly appealing.

Yet Breckinridge also knew himself. He wanted to be part of the creation of the new Southern nation, just as his grandfather and great-grandfather had helped build the new American republic after it had won independence from Britain. He thought of all the difficult tasks that needed to be done, from rebuilding the Southern rail lines to creating a Confederate Supreme Court. He knew that the South needed men like him to lay the foundations for the future. Was it not his duty to remain in public life?

Breckinridge refocused his attention on the meeting when Reagan cleared his throat to speak.

"Neither we nor the Yankees have yet mentioned the Indian Territory," the Texan observed.

Breckinridge was slightly taken aback, having almost forgotten about that subject. Reagan, being only man from the Trans-Mississippi at the talks, had obviously not. The loosely organized region just north of Texas, to which the United States had exiled thousands of Indians during the days of Andrew Jackson, was being fought over between the various tribes, some of which had pledged loyalty to the Confederacy while others had maintained an allegiance to the Union.

"I'm not in favor of giving anything up to the Yankees," Miles said. "But I must admit that the Indian Territory is not high on my list of priorities."

"My friends back home are concerned about it," Reagan replied. "They stress the need for the Territory to come under Confederate control in order to serve as a buffer between the Yankees in Kansas and our settlements in Texas."

"I think bringing such a messy place into the Confederacy might be more trouble than it's worth," Breckinridge said.

"I'm inclined to agree," Miles said. "More to the point, I would say that the fewer Indians in the Confederacy, the better. They can't be citizens, nor have they historically made good slaves. Better not to have to deal with them. The Confederacy is and must remain a nation for the white man."

Breckinridge found Miles's words distasteful, for he respected Indians and considered them, despite their very different cultures, fully the equal of white men. Yet he knew that most Southern men held the same view of Indians as Miles.

"Would it not be reasonable to let the Indians in the Territory simply go their own way?" Stephens asked. "Perhaps an independent state of some sort would make a more effective buffer between our respective Western territories. If we gain control of the territory, we merely move the point of contact with the Yankees farther north."

Breckinridge shook his head. "An independent state might seek some sort of relationship with a foreign power," he said. "The Indians spent centuries playing the English, French, and Spanish off against one another, you know. The French have been working to gain control of Mexico for the past few years. I would not like to see them active farther north."

"That's true," Stephens agreed. "We would have to hold some sort of protectorate over it, as Britain does with many states around the world."

Breckinridge thought for a moment of his new British friend, Garnet Wolseley, who was likely to have traveled through many of those protectorates during his service in the

British army. Perhaps he might have some insight into how such an arrangement might work. He resolved to ask Wolseley about it when they met up for their whiskey.

The discussion went back and forth for some time. As he listened, Breckinridge noted that none of the delegates referred to the Confederate claims for Missouri or West Virginia. In their minds, those states had already been lost and weren't worth talking about. Moreover, discussions of the referendum in Maryland were limited to its use as a negotiating tool; no one believed that the Yankees would actually allow such a vote to take place. All eyes were fixed firmly on the need to keep control of the whole of Louisiana and regain control of Tennessee. He wished the others shared his convictions regarding Kentucky.

Stephens looked at the grandfather clock that ticked away on one of the room's walls. "It is time for us to rejoin our Northern friends. Are we ready?"

*   *   *   *   *

"I hope I am being clear when I say that there is no chance whatsoever of a referendum in Maryland on whether they shall join the Confederacy," Seymour said. His voice sounded tired and frustrated, for they had been going back and forth on the question for more than an hour. "It is not on the table. It is no more likely than us ceding control of Rhode Island. The sooner you accept this, the sooner we can move on to other matters."

"But we have stated our willingness to allow a referendum in Louisiana," Stephens objected. "Why not extend the same courtesy to Maryland?"

"For obvious reasons!" Porter replied, irritated. "If Maryland were to become a Confederate state, Washington City would be surrounded by enemy territory! You see this as clearly as I do!"

"Well, if you refuse to accommodate us on the question of Maryland, we shall withdraw our agreement to allow a referendum in Louisiana," Stephens said simply.

"I, in turn, remind you that New Orleans is occupied by Union troops," Seymour countered. "The majority of the population of Louisiana currently lives under Union authority."

Stephens sat back, appearing increasingly aggravated. Breckinridge wasn't sure if his frustration was genuine or a calculated ploy. The talks had focused on Maryland and Louisiana, with no one mentioning the even more delicate topic of Tennessee. Did this indicate that the Yankees were more willing to hold a plebiscite there, or would they be as firm on that question as they were being on Maryland? Kentucky had also not yet been mentioned, to Breckinridge's dismay.

At least the issue of the Indian Territory had been settled quickly and to mutual satisfaction. With Reagan doing most of the talking for the Southern side, it had been agreed that the Indian Territory would be an independent state under some sort of mutual protectorate of both the Union and the Confederacy. The details, it had been agreed, could be worked out later. Everyone was pleased with the arrangement, for a buffer state between the western lands of both countries was in the interests of everybody.

Breckinridge was also pleased for another reason. Although he had been as strong a proponent of westward expansion as any man before the war, he had always been troubled by the knowledge that the price paid for American progress was the destruction of the Indian way of life and the loss of their freedom. If the Indians were given their own state, to govern as they pleased, perhaps the conscience of the whites could be soothed. Such philosophical musings, however, were for another time.

The status of the New Mexico Territory had also been settled, albeit not as easily. The Confederate delegation had been instructed by Jefferson Davis to attempt to secure New Mexico as Confederate territory, but even Postmaster Reagan, the staunchest Davis supporter among them, had quickly concluded that this was impossible. Porter and Hamlin had laughed when Stephens had brought the issue up. Since Confederate troops had been driven from New Mexico in 1862, the region had been firmly under Union control. As Secretary of War, Breckinridge knew that the South had no ability whatsoever to send forces into the area. The Confederates had therefore surrendered all claims to the region.

Thus had quietly died the dream of a Southern-controlled transcontinental railroad, Breckinridge silently reflected. It had been the goal of a generation of Southern politicians in Washington City and the various state capitals. Breckinridge knew that they would come in for a great deal of criticism when the treaty was published in the Southern newspapers, but what could be done about it?

Another issue that had been settled with surprising ease was that of free navigation of the Mississippi River. The Northerners had insisted that their cargo vessels face no obstacles, whether in terms of outright obstruction or by indirect means such as monetary tolls, when traveling the river from Union territory down to the Gulf of Mexico. This was critical for the United States, as the Mississippi River was the primary conduit for the agricultural produce of the Great Plains to reach the markets of Europe and Latin America. It had been decided that, for all legal purposes, vessels of the United States would be treated no differently than vessels of the Confederate States.

Breckinridge had insisted that military vessels be excluded from any such liberties when traveling down the Mississippi River. The Union delegates, who could devise no reasonable argument against such a proposition, had agreed. The issue had thus been settled. Granting the North free navigation of the Mississippi cost the Confederacy nothing and the commerce that would be fostered would be good for the South as well as the North.

But if the Indian Territory, the New Mexico Territory, and free navigation of the Mississippi River had been easily dealt with, the question of holding referendums in the disputed states was proving much more contentious than Breckinridge had expected.

Miles, who had remained rather quiet, suddenly broke into the conversation. "If you are unwilling to allow a plebiscite in Maryland out of fear for the security of Washington City, perhaps you might allow one in Kentucky instead?" He glanced at Breckinridge quickly after saying these words.

Hamlin scowled. "You must be joking."

Seymour shook his head. "There is no more chance for a plebiscite in Kentucky than there is in Maryland. Aside from raids, no Confederate troops have set foot on Kentucky soil since we chased out Bragg's army in October of 1862."

"Thousands of Kentucky soldiers serve in the Confederate Army," Miles said forcefully. "One of them is sitting with us here at this table. I don't think there is much question that the spirit of the Kentucky people is with the Confederacy."

Breckinridge wondered for a moment why Congressman Miles had brought the issue up so suddenly. He had contributed comparatively little to the debates unless the issues under discussion had involved slavery, content to let Stephens and himself do most of the talking.

"Far more Kentuckians served in the Union army than the rebel forces," Seymour countered. "They rejected secession at the beginning of the war. The state legislature is strongly unionist."

"Were the elections for that legislature free and fair?" Miles asked. "I frankly don't think so."

"The secessionists boycotted the election!" Hamlin replied quickly. "Is that the fault of the United States? No. It's because they knew they were going to lose."

"Events of the past are irrelevant," Breckinridge interjected forcefully, deciding that the issue required his participation. "What matters is what the people of Kentucky think today, and I believe that the sympathies of the people of Kentucky are now with the Confederacy more than the Union. Considering the suffering the state has endured through four years of war, I believe they deserve the opportunity to express their views through a vote."

The Union delegates were silent for a moment. As the most prominent man of Kentucky, North or South, Breckinridge's views on the question commanded respect. Still, he was not so naïve as to think this would have an impact on the outcome of the discussion.

Seymour spoke carefully. "What makes you think the people of Kentucky have any greater desire to join the Confederacy now than they did in 1861? They could have seceded when the other slave states did, but they chose to remain loyal to the Union."

"They have watched as their rights have been trampled upon by the Union government," Breckinridge replied. "They've seen their young men conscripted to make war on their fellow Southerners. They've seen their taxes raised to exorbitant heights and their crops and livestock confiscated. They've seen newspapers shut down and many of their most prominent citizens arrested simply for opposing the war. General Stephen Burbridge, the Union commander in Kentucky, has become known as 'Butcher Burbridge' for his ruthless military rule, which has seen Confederate sympathizers publicly executed on trumped-up charges. Why should they continue to support a government that treats them so harshly?"

"Say what you want, John," Hamlin responded. "But we are not about to allow another state to be torn from the Union on the basis of Confederate propaganda."

Breckinridge drew his head back in surprise. "It's not propaganda," he protested. "All of what I just said is well known to be the truth."

"Everyone has suffered during the war," Seymour replied. "If one takes your logic to its obvious conclusion, every single state should be given a referendum on whether to join the Union or the Confederacy. We all saw the disaster caused by Stephen Douglas's doctrine of popular sovereignty before the war, when the new territories were allowed to vote on whether to allow slavery in their borders. Do we want to see every state, North and South, turned into another Bleeding Kansas? I say no. Enough blood has already been shed."

"Fine words, Governor," Miles replied sardonically. "But I'm afraid our position has not changed. We still expect a plebiscite to be held in either Maryland or Kentucky, if not both. And Tennessee, too, of course."

"Plebiscites will not be considered for either Maryland or Kentucky," Seymour said firmly.

"In that case, we retract our offer of a plebiscite in Louisiana," Stephens said with satisfaction.

Breckinridge wondered for a moment what had pleased Stephens, then instantly realized it. When he had specified that referendums would never be held in Maryland or Kentucky, Seymour had notably failed to mention Tennessee. Did this mean that the Yankees were now willing to hold a vote in that state, which they had previously been unwilling to do? If so, the Confederates would have obtained one of their key objectives in the talks. Any such vote would surely favor the Confederates, Unionist support in the eastern part of the state notwithstanding.

The haggling went on for another hour. Breckinridge grew increasingly impatient and frustrated as the Northerners continually insisted on a referendum in Louisiana while refusing to accept any plebiscite in either Maryland or Kentucky. The Southerners remained adamant on the exact opposite position. It was obvious that the talks were going nowhere. Breckinridge began feeling the strong desire to have a bourbon.

"It is almost seven," Seymour finally said, looking over at the clock. "Since we are not getting anything accomplished on the issue of plebiscites, I suggest that we close the talks for the evening and reconvene in the morning."

"I have no objection in principle," Stephens said immediately. "However, as a courtesy I would like to inform the Union commissioners that tomorrow we will be bringing up the question of reparations."

"Reparations?" Black asked, a confused look on his face.

"The Confederacy is of the opinion that, considering the tremendous damage to civilian property caused by the Union army and the economic distress caused by the blockade, the United States should pay financial compensation to the Confederate government."

Hamlin laughed out loud. "You really expect us to pay you money?" he exclaimed. "You were the ones who left the Union. You were the ones who started the war by firing on Fort Sumter. And now you have the gall to demand money from us, like some low criminal on the street?"

"We don't want to argue over the cause of the war or whose fault it was," Breckinridge said. "But the fact is that the Union army waged war against the civilian population of the Confederacy in violation of all the customs of civilized nations. Many of the towns and farms in the Shenandoah Valley, where I myself served, were burned by your troops. Much of Mississippi was left in ruins during Sherman's campaign against Meridian. Grant's army bombarded Atlanta with heavy artillery during his attempt to capture it, causing many civilian casualties. These are only a few examples."

"The Confederacy also waged war on the civilian population of the North," Black said. "Countless towns and farms in Missouri were ransacked by Southern partisan ranger units. Jubal Early's men burned the city of Chambersburg to the ground. John Hunt Morgan's men looted their way across hundreds of miles during their 1863 raid through Indiana and Ohio. Like you, I can cite numerous other examples."

"I don't disagree," Breckinridge said with sincerity. "Men on both sides were guilty of unwarranted destruction of private property. But any impartial observer can see that the wrongs of the Union in this regard vastly outweigh the wrongs of the Confederacy."

"Only because your armies lacked the ability to invade our territory, except through raids and brief incursions," Hamlin countered. "Had Lee won the Battle of Gettysburg, I am sure the towns and farms of Pennsylvania would have been treated no differently by your men than those in the Shenandoah Valley were treated by ours."

"What might have happened is irrelevant," Breckinridge replied. "We are concerned here only with what did happen."

Black spoke next. "If it is money we are going to be discussing tomorrow, we should talk about how large a proportion of the prewar national debt of the United States is going to be assumed by the Confederacy."

Stephens glanced knowingly at Breckinridge, acknowledging his prescience on this question. It was Miles, however, who responded for the Southern delegation.

"I see no reason for the Confederacy to assume a penny of the prewar national debt. Virtually the whole national budget before the war went to internal improvements in the North. Canals, roads, and such. The South never asked for such assistance and never wanted it."

"Nonsense," Hamlin spat. "You Southerners made a lot of loud noise protesting the funding of internal improvements, but that didn't stop your congressional representatives from quietly begging for them behind the scenes whenever appropriation bills came onto the floor."

Breckinridge didn't appreciate Hamlin's insulting tone, but he couldn't deny the truth of what he said. As a congressional representative for Kentucky, Breckinridge had decried internal improvements in many campaign speeches, but had also made sure that his home state and district got their share of the money when the cards came down.

Seymour was talking. "Besides, a considerable chunk of federal revenue did not go to internal improvements. The military expenditure is the most obvious source of spending and it was equally beneficial to North and South. The diplomatic establishments around the world were paid for with federal funds, and they also benefited both North and South."

Porter broke in. "Don't forget the construction of coastal fortifications. The very forts which you Southerners used to defend your own ports and cities against us were built by the federal government."

"Since the North saw fit to attempt to hold the South in the Union by force of arms, I see no reason why any of this should matter," Miles said.

Seymour smiled smugly. "It seems to me that you Southerners wish to have the benefits of independence without assuming any of the responsibilities. You're acting rather like the young man who seeks to be free of his father's control but still writes letters home begging for money."

Stephens leaned forward. "We have understood your position, gentlemen. I hope that you have understood ours. As Mr. Seymour has said, it is now late and we should conclude for the day. Tired men, after all, are apt to become irritated."

"Very well," Seymour said. "We shall reconvene tomorrow morning to continue our discussion of borders and plebiscites, with these two financial questions on the table as well. Is there any objection?"

"None at all," Stephens said.

As the commissioners rose from their chairs and exchanged handshakes, Breckinridge reflected on how exhausting and acrimonious the first day had been. He prayed that the succeeding days would be less so, though he doubted

72

his prayer would be answered. In any event, he was eager to get to the bar at the Rossin House Hotel.

Chapter Three

Breckinridge sat alone at the bar, cradling an ornate glass filled with Armagnac. The bartender had told him that it was a French brandy and had strongly recommended it. Though he had come to the bar intending to indulge in bourbon, Breckinridge had to admit that the Armagnac was wonderful. The bartender obviously knew what he was talking about.

His colleagues had all gone their own ways. Stephens had expressed a desire to write a letter to his brother Linton, with whom he was particularly close. Reagan had been assigned the task of composing a brief report to be sent by telegraph to President Davis the next day, detailing the Union delegation's initial terms. Miles had made a vague remark about being tired, but Breckinridge had seen him stroll out onto the street twenty minutes earlier. Considering the rumors about the South Carolina congressman that circulated in Richmond parlors, Breckinridge assumed Miles had gone hunting for female companionship.

Happy to have some time alone, Breckinridge reflected on the events of the day. He was pleased with how easy it had been to deal with the issues of the Indian Territory, the New Mexico Territory, and free navigation of the Mississippi River. When it came to the border states, however, the talks seemed destined for an eternal stalemate. The two sides had spent hours simply repeating their respective positions to one another. Breckinridge remembered the Greek tale of Sisyphus, the man condemned by the gods to roll a giant boulder up to the top of a hill in the underworld, only to have the boulder roll down again as soon as the task was completed, thus damning him to repeat the chore over and over again for all eternity.

In retrospect, Breckinridge thought it had perhaps been a mistake not to press the Yankees on the status of Missouri and West Virginia. Neither state was going to end up in the Confederacy, of course. Moreover, Breckinridge wouldn't have wanted either of them. West Virginians generally were loyal to the Union and Missouri was a bloody, anarchic mess. No good and much evil would have come from incorporating those states into the Confederacy. But had the Southern delegation not simply given in on those two states, they might have been able to press the Yankees harder on the case of Tennessee and Kentucky. They would, in a sense, have had more chips to play with.

On the other hand, Breckinridge thought that Stephens had made a brilliant move by expressing a willingness to hold a plebiscite in Louisiana. He knew that Davis would be outraged by such a suggestion and that it would be criticized in many Southern newspapers, but Breckinridge was confident that such a vote would go the Confederacy's way. Despite years of Union occupation, the people of New Orleans had remained, by all accounts, staunchly loyal to the Confederacy. It was a risk, but hopefully not a serious one.

By giving in on Louisiana and continuing to push hard on Maryland and Kentucky, the Confederate bargaining position on Tennessee had been greatly strengthened. Breckinridge had slowly begun to believe that the Yankees always intended to agree to a plebiscite in Tennessee and were only trying to hold the line to make sure the Confederates gave concessions on other issues. The question on his mind was whether the Yankees might agree to a referendum in Kentucky if the South dropped its demand for a vote in Maryland.

He was troubled by the intense acrimony that had characterized the morning's discussion of slavery, which had been instigated by Miles. These questions had been tactfully overlooked during the afternoon's session, but Breckinridge knew that they would surely crop up again the next day. Congressman Miles was not helping matters by his stridency. If Miles continued to push forcefully with his demands for the return of freed slaves, the enslavement of captured black soldiers, and the inclusion of a treaty provision for the return of fugitive slaves, the talks might well collapse. Even if Miles somehow waved a magic wand and succeeded in getting those provisions into the treaty, the Republican-controlled Senate would surely reject ratification. The result would be a long, legal limbo between the North and South or perhaps even a resumption of the war.

In his heart, Breckinridge was no friend of slavery. Granting the North the concessions it was demanding on slavery was, Breckinridge thought, simple common sense. It would not only help the process of ratification, but might engender sufficient goodwill on the part of the Northern delegation to induce them to give in on the issue of a plebiscite in Tennessee and, just possibly, Kentucky.

He asked himself if there was any real chance that the Union delegation would allow a referendum in Kentucky. He couldn't be certain, but Breckinridge thought that the Northerners were slightly less obstinate on Kentucky than on Maryland. That gave him a glimmer of hope, though only a faint one. At no point during the war had the Confederacy been in complete control of Kentucky. If it were to join the Confederacy, the United States would be faced with a potential military threat to Ohio, Indiana, and Illinois. Were he in the Union delegation's place, Breckinridge knew he would never countenance a plebiscite.

Even if a referendum were to be held, Breckinridge knew that the vote might not be in the Confederacy's favor. Northern sympathizers had been strong enough to prevent the state from seceding in 1861. Despite some public displays of welcome, relatively few Kentuckians had joined the Confederate army during Bragg's ill-fated invasion in 1862. Breckinridge's keen political instincts told him that the Confederacy had a less-than-even chance of winning any plebiscite. Nobody knew the voting habits of Kentuckians better than he did.

Yet, his heart still yearned for Kentucky to be brought into the Confederacy. In 1861, once it had become clear that his own efforts to keep the Union together had become futile, Breckinridge had given himself body and soul to the Confederate cause. He had served the cause both as a soldier and as a politician. But his blood was in the Bluegrass State. If Kentucky did not join the Confederacy, could he ever truly feel at home in the new country?

He thought again of his own future prospects, which would be greatly impacted by the fate of Kentucky. If he did indeed choose to retire from public life, he'd rather resume his law practice in Lexington than in Richmond. He wished for his children to come of age in their own native land. On the other hand, if he did intend to continue his political career, where would he find a constituency? He was popular throughout the South, but if he chose to run for Congress from Virginia, Tennessee, or some other state, he might encounter fierce opposition from the local political leadership, who might not be keen on being represented by an outsider.

Of course, there was always the possibility that could put himself forward to be Jefferson Davis's successor in 1867. Countless newspapers had speculated that he would be a natural choice for the highest office in the land. If he did decide to devote himself to laying strong and solid foundations for the newly independent Confederacy, what better way to do this than as its chief executive?

While either Robert E. Lee or Joseph Johnston could probably have the presidency if they wanted it, Breckinridge knew that neither man had any interest in politics. Lee, for one, was a tired man in increasingly ill health. Just two months earlier, while dining at Breckinridge's house in Richmond, the great general had told Breckinridge how political ambition had ruined his father's life and that he had no intention of meeting the same fate. For his part, Johnston seemed content to enjoy the social prestige won by his victories at Atlanta and Fairburn and make disparaging remarks about Jefferson Davis at Richmond cocktail parties.

But if neither Lee nor Johnston were to be candidates, who then would be the man to succeed Davis? Perhaps James Longstreet? Or Wade Hampton? Breckinridge assumed that Miles and his fellow Fire-Eaters would try to sponsor a candidate that they could manipulate for their own purposes. That was a disquieting prospect.

He raised his glass of Armagnac to his lips. The hot feel of the fortified wine as it splashed down his throat was comforting. He had had enough alcohol that he was pleasantly relaxed, though not so much that his cognitive powers were diminished. He was not sure whether he would have another before retiring. That decision could wait until he had finished the glass in his hand.

"May I join you, General Breckinridge?"

He turned to see Garnet Wolseley standing beside his barstool. It was a pleasant surprise.

"By all means, Colonel. I could use the company, in fact. Your first drink shall be on me."

"And your next shall therefore be on me," Wolseley said with a smile as he slid onto the adjoining barstool. "What are you drinking?"

"The bartender says it is called Armagnac. I am enjoying it very much."

"Armagnac is very nice," Wolseley said. "I shall have one as well." He motioned to the bartender and gestured towards Breckinridge's drink. The man wordlessly nodded.

"You have had it before, then?" Breckinridge asked.

"Many times. Brandy is my drink of choice, as it is for most officers in the British army. No British regiment would go on campaign without a sufficient supply of brandy of some kind. Except for the Highlanders, of course, who insist on bringing along their scotch."

"Scotch?"

"Whiskey made in Scotland. I have been given some on occasion by Scottish officers. It is very good. I am not sure you would rank it with your bourbon, but you should try it if given the chance." The bartender handed Wolseley his drink. "What shall we drink to, General?" the Englishman asked. "Confusion to our enemies, perhaps?"

Breckinridge chuckled. "At this point, I would rather they have more wisdom than confusion. Why don't we drink to fallen comrades?"

"I'll drink to that."

Their glasses clinked. Breckinridge motioned to the bartender for another.

"How are the talks progressing?" Wolseley asked politely.

"We have agreed not to discuss the specifics outside of the conference room," Breckinridge said. "I suppose I can tell you that this first day has left me exhausted and somewhat disillusioned."

"I have no political stuff in me," Wolseley said simply. "I am a soldier and nothing else. Tell me where the enemy is so that I may attack him. That's all that interests me."

"I wish I could be so fortunate," Breckinridge answered ruefully. "You never consider the political implications of the wars in which you have fought?"

"Not at all," Wolseley answered simply. "What would be the point? The men against whom I have fought were the enemies of Her Majesty Queen Victoria. That was enough for me."

"Not once?"

Wolseley considered the question a bit more carefully. "Perhaps in India during the Sepoy Mutiny. The mutineers, dastardly and ungrateful fellows, had killed British women and children. That needed to be avenged immediately and without mercy. And we avenged them, by God! It upset me also that these mutineers tried to overthrow the political structure we British had so carefully built in India over a century, bringing enlightenment and civilization to the dark peoples of the Subcontinent. It was as if they had shattered a precious china vase."

Breckinridge thought for a moment about the Fire-Eaters. In pushing for secession for so long and making compromise in Washington all but impossible, they had shattered a precious china vase, too. That was all in the past now, though. What was done was done.

Wolseley sipped his brandy and continued. "I suppose, if I really thought about it, I could say that I fight to expand the benefits to mankind that the British Empire brings. Good government, the Christian religion, education, sound economic practices, all that sort of thing. But I don't think about such things too much, to be perfectly honest. Soldiers should focus on war."

"I envy you," Breckinridge said with a smile. "I think about such things far too much. It wears on one's mind."

"I don't see why," Wolseley replied. "You Confederates fight for a cause which is not complicated. You live your life a certain way, including your own particular way of regulating the relationship between the white and black races. The Union, led by the tyrant Lincoln, was trying to force its own view of how such things should be done upon you. You fought them. You won. What more is there to think about, my good fellow?"

Breckinridge found himself envying Wolseley all the more as he listened to these words. How liberating it would be to never have to consider the point of view of one's opponent, or to be able to ignore the human suffering caused by one's exploitation of other human beings for economic gain. The British, at least, rationalized their mistreatment of the natives of India with the excuse that they were bringing the benefits of

Western civilization and Christianity to the Subcontinent. Southerners, by contrast, made little effort to hide the brutality of slavery.

He overlooked Wolseley's comment about Lincoln being a tyrant. Despite their political differences and the fact that they were opponents in the 1860 election, Breckinridge and Lincoln had a warm personal friendship, helped by the fact that Mary Todd Lincoln was Breckinridge's cousin. Breckinridge assumed that Wolseley would find this confusing and decided not to bring it up.

He then changed the subject. "Why have you been posted to Canada, Colonel?"

A look of irritation crossed Wolseley's face. "I've been in Canada for three-and-a-half years," he said sourly. "You recall back in 1861, when the Yankees had the gall to insult the British flag by stopping one of our ships on the high seas?"

"The Trent Affair. Of course I remember."

"I was one of the commanders of the troops sent over from Britain to reinforce the Canadian frontier in the event of war between the United States and the British Empire. War was averted, as you know, when Lincoln gave in and issued an apology to Her Majesty's government. I was disappointed, I must say, for I was eager to see action against the Americans. It would have been very interesting, I think."

"Certainly the war would have been shortened, saving many lives," Breckinridge observed.

Wolseley shrugged and went on. "I have been here ever since, training the Canadian militia. It's a lovely country, to be sure. Great hunting. But I find it terribly boring most of the time. I yearn for action once again." He stopped for a moment to take a sip of brandy. "Of course, there's this trouble with the Fenians."

"Fenians?"

"Irish extremists who seek to detach Ireland from the British Empire. An idiotic notion, I know. But there are apparently several thousand of them in the United States. Many of them served in the Union Army, just to gain military experience. Now, rumor has it, they intend to launch raids from the territory of the United States into Canada. If the United States government allows this to happen, war would be a serious possibility."

Breckinridge recalled hearing about the Fenians in the newspapers. He had not given the reports much credit, but obviously they were in earnest enough for Wolseley to take them seriously. It would be foolish for the McClellan administration to allow the Fenians to conduct their activities from United States soil. Then again, the Irish immigrant population in the major cities was one of the Democratic Party's most important voting blocs and McClellan relied on them for much of his support.

"Of course, there are prospects for action elsewhere," Wolseley said. "British forces are fighting somewhere in the world almost every month of every year. Africa, China, the Northwest Frontier of India. If war does not break out between the Empire and the United States, perhaps I might seek more laurels elsewhere."

"I'm sure you have already won plenty of laurels."

"Truth, truth. But then, so have you. Tell me, what was the Battle of Shiloh like?"

The two men spent the next hour describing their respective battles and campaigns. Breckinridge told Wolseley of the carnage at Shiloh, the confused street fighting at Baton Rouge, the ferocious combat at Murfreesboro and Chickamauga, and the disgraceful rout at Missionary Ridge. He described his service in the Shenandoah Valley, the terrible battle at Cold Harbor, and his exhilarating service as second-in-command to Jubal Early during the celebrated raid on Washington City. He ended his discourse with a description of the bloody battles against Sheridan's army in the months just before the ceasefire had brought an end to the fighting.

Wolseley's exploits were just as thrilling and certainly more exotic. He told of his baptism of fire in a campaign in the malarial country known as Burma, his service against the Russians at the Siege of Sevastopol during the Crimean War, and his participation in the famous Relief of Lucknow during the Indian Mutiny. Most fascinating to Breckinridge was Wolseley's tale of the campaign against the Emperor of China during the Second Opium War in 1860.

Listening to Wolseley as he described his adventures in faraway lands, Breckinridge felt the tug of wanderlust. He yearned to see Europe, to walk through the cathedrals of England and France, to see the ruins of Rome, to set foot on the islands of the Aegean. He had been reading about these magical places since he had been a boy. Yet Wolseley spoke of even more distant lands, where civilization as Breckinridge understood it was vastly different and more fascinating. He wondered if he would ever be able to visit such places as India or China.

Perhaps he would get his chance soon enough. When the conference was over, he could serve out the rest of his time as Secretary of War and then retire from public life forever if he so wished. Once he resumed his law practice, using his reputation to attract wealthy clients, it shouldn't be too difficult to build up a sufficient fortune after a few years to travel the world as he liked. His heart jumped at the thought of walking with his wife Mary through the streets of London and Paris. But if he turned his back on politics, would that leave the Fire-Eaters free to raise their own man to the presidency?

He realized his mind was beginning to wander from the conversation and he refocused. "When we arrived, Mayor Medcalf said you belonged to the Perthshire Light Infantry?"

Wolseley took another sip of Armagnac. "Yes. Our official designation is the 90th Regiment of Foot."

"But that regiment is not here in Toronto, is it?"

"No, they are currently on garrison duty back in England. The men are very bored, according to the letters I receive from my brother officers. The fact that they are jealous of me, as I am out here in this tedious country, tells you something of how exciting life must be in the regimental encampment. They are eager for action."

"Why do they not join another regiment, then? A unit soon to be deployed where fighting is likely."

Wolseley looked at Breckinridge in surprise. "A man could no more leave his regiment to join another than he could leave his family to join another."

"Really?"

"Heavens, no! Once a soldier has made a decision as to which regiment he shall spend his service in, it is almost impossible for him to change his mind. What would become of the various regiments if men could simply abandon them whenever they choose?"

"You take your regimental identities seriously, do you?"

"More seriously than anything, except perhaps horse racing. Each regiment is like its own little community that wanders around the world fighting the Queen's enemies. Each has its own peculiar traditions and has different friendships and animosities with other regiments. Each regiment celebrates anniversaries of great battles from its past history, some going back centuries. It's all delightful, of course. But it plays a very important role in building a unique cohesion and élan that makes the British regiment the most formidable military unit in the world."

"Our units have only existed a few years," Breckinridge replied. "But they already have distinctive identities. I commanded the Orphan Brigade, so-called because it was made up of Kentucky soldiers in Confederate service. Since Kentucky never seceded, the men couldn't go home and saw themselves as orphans. Other units stand out, too. The Stonewall Brigade, Cockrell's Missouri Brigade, the Louisiana Tigers."

"Perhaps those unique unit identities are a foundation on which you can build the peacetime Confederate army," Wolseley said. "After all, there is always the possibility of another war between your nation and the United States. If that happens, your army will need to be ready."

"And as the Secretary of War, it is my job to make it so," Breckinridge said just before taking another sip of brandy. He said a silent prayer to God that peace would always prevail between the people of the North and South.

"You look tired," Wolseley observed.

"What? Oh, not at all!"

"It's all right, old boy. You've had a very long day. I've kept you here too long."

"I am tired," Breckinridge admitted. "But I have greatly enjoyed our conversation. I probably should retire, though. Tomorrow will likely be as long as today."

"Very well. Do not forget to inform me of the future schedule of the conference, so that I may arrange our excursion to the battlefield at Quebec. That is, if you are still interested."

"Of course I am. Aside perhaps from Cortez conquering Tenochtitlan, no more important event ever took place in North America than the British capture of Quebec. To visit the battlefield in the company of such a distinguished soldier as yourself would be a truly memorable occasion."

"Well, then, in that case I bid you a good evening and a pleasant night's sleep." Wolseley put his glass on the bar, slid off the barstool, and put a banknote down on the bar. He clapped Breckinridge a few times on the shoulder and took his leave. Breckinridge, who still had a few sips of brandy remaining in his glass, pondered his new British friend for a few moments. His conversation with Wolseley had been a pleasant intermission from the pressures of the peace conference, but it was time for him to turn his thoughts once again towards the work at hand.

*   *   *   *   *

The second and third days of negotiation proved to be as rancorous and exasperating as the first day, leaving Breckinridge greatly discouraged. The fourth day, however, started with a shock.

"I'm sorry?" Stephens said, leaning forward over the table. "Could you please repeat that?"

"Fort Monroe in Virginia and Fort Pickens and Key West in Florida," Seymour said. "They have never been occupied by the Confederacy. We therefore expect that they shall remain the property of the United States government."

"Surely you must be joking," Stephens replied.

"No, not at all."

"Those forts are vital for the defense of the Confederacy," Breckinridge interjected. "Obviously you have to understand that they must devolve to our control."

Seymour shrugged. "The defense of the Confederacy is your problem, not ours. As I said, they have never been held by Confederate forces. I see no more reason for us to give them to you than for us to give you Fort Warren in Boston Harbor."

The military man in Breckinridge instantly found himself analyzing the consequences of those key military posts remaining in Union hands. Fort Monroe controlled the entrance to Hampton Roads, and with it access to the key naval base at Norfolk and the James and York Rivers that led up to Richmond. Fort Pickens controlled access to the crucial port of Pensacola. Key West had provided a secure Union naval base for the blockade of both the Gulf Coast and the lower Atlantic Coast. By holding on to these fortifications, the United States would have the ability to restore the naval blockade without much trouble.

Stephens turned to Breckinridge. As the military representative of the commission, it was his responsibility to argue their case on an issue such as this.

"You cannot expect us to acquiesce to this proposal, Mr. Seymour," Breckinridge began. "If the United States maintains control over those places, it would be like a noose drawn around the South's neck, ready to be tightened whenever you want."

"I rather like that image," Hamlin said with an uncharacteristic grin.

"Well, we shall not accept it."

"I am very sorry to hear that," Seymour said. "Our instructions are that we cannot negotiate on this point."

It was a ploy, Breckinridge saw instantly. Seymour had never hinted towards being bound by his instructions in such a manner before. By making such an unlikely claim, he had gone just a bit too far and tipped his hand.

"You'd better reread your instructions then," Miles said dryly. "And you might want to leave your reading glasses on the table when you do so. Because your demand to keep those forts represents an infringement on our sovereignty, which we cannot abide."

"Perhaps we could leave this issue on the table," Breckinridge recommended. He foresaw that the Yankees would drop it soon enough and did not want to allow the day to fall into meaningless rancor, as had happened the past few days. "We might return to it tomorrow, after we have had a chance to discuss it among ourselves."

"Certainly," Seymour said in an agreeable tone.

"What's next?" Stephens asked.

Seymour sat upright and stiffened slightly in his chair. He turned to Hamlin and nodded.

"We would like to open a discussion on the issue of atrocities," the former Vice President said.

"Atrocities?" Reagan asked.

"Yes. During the course of the war, on many occasions, Confederate soldiers committed atrocities against Union soldiers, particularly those units composed of black troops. We believe that the soldiers and officers responsible for these vile acts must be held accountable."

Breckinridge felt an unpleasant tightening in his stomach. War, even under the best of circumstances, was a nasty business. There was, however, a difference between disciplined men fighting one another in regular battles and brutal men slaughtering unarmed or wounded men as though they were helpless animals. Sadly, the latter had happened more than once during the war and the victims had almost always been black Union troops. The most notable case had been the massacre of the Union garrison at Fort Pillow by troops under Nathan Bedford Forrest, but it had also happened at the Battle of the Crater on the Petersburg front, at the Battle of Olustee in Florida, and in other locations.

Troops under Breckinridge's direct control had never carried out any such killings, but one officer under his command had done so. When he had commanded the department of southwestern Virginia, during the murky time between the unofficial ceasefire in November of 1864 and the official armistice in March of 1865, a cavalry colonel named Felix Robertson had fought a large skirmish near the town of Honaker with a force of Union infantry composed of black troops. The Southerners had won, but the victory had been tarnished by stories that Robertson's troops had wandered the battlefield the following morning, searching for wounded black troops who were still alive and then ruthlessly killing them with sabers.

The massacre perpetuated by Robertson and his men had been, in a way, even worse than the killings that had taken place at Fort Pillow. In the latter, according to the accounts Breckinridge had read, the men had essentially gone berserk in the midst of battle or its immediate aftermath. At Honaker, however, the battle had been over for hours and the men had even had some sleep before they had moved forward with the clear intention of murdering blacks in cold blood.

Breckinridge had been horrified when this had been reported to him and he had immediately ordered Robertson's arrest. When President Davis had asked him to assume the post of Secretary of War, Breckinridge had insisted that Robertson be cashiered and dismissed from the service before he had accepted the post. Breckinridge hoped that Robertson would be tried and convicted in a court of law, but the man had subsequently disappeared. Rumor placed him on the road to Texas.

Miles responded to Hamlin first. "These stories of atrocities against blacks are nothing but abolitionist propaganda. Why would we want to destroy valuable slave property? I'm rather surprised that a man of your intelligence would be so gullible."

Hamlin turned towards Breckinridge. "Is that so, Mr. Breckinridge? Are these reports merely propaganda?"

He waited a moment before replying. He did not want to appear to be standing on the side of the Northern delegation against Miles, but his sense of honesty refused to let him speak a blatant untruth. "There were many unfortunate incidents during the war, I'm sad to say."

"What exactly is the United States proposing?" Stephens said, clearly wanting to cut to the heart of the matter.

"It's very simple, actually," Hamlin replied. "We demand that the men who committed these atrocities be handed over to the United States."

Breckinridge shook his head. "That we cannot allow."

"Why not?" Hamlin asked. "You yourself admit many of these killings took place. You are a man of honor, Mr. Breckinridge. How can you protect murderers?"

He glanced at Porter. "General Porter and I are the two men at this table who have experienced the horrors of this war directly. When speaking of battles involving thousands of confused and terrified men trying to kill or be killed, one cannot treat the situation in the same way as one would an ordinary crime."

Seymour glanced over at his colleagues a moment before turning to Breckinridge again. "We don't wish to appear unreasonable, of course. We recognize the unfortunate impossibility of bringing all the killers to justice. We therefore limit our demand to those officers in command of the troops who carried out the massacres in question."

Reagan leaned forward and made a rare foray into the deliberations. "Surely you must see the fairness of reciprocity. We shall insist that the Union hand over to the Confederacy those men who deliberately starved Confederate prisoners at Point Lookout in Maryland, the Elmira prison camp in New York, and other locations."

Porter grimaced. "We could add to our demands the Confederate officers in charge at Andersonville and half a dozen other prison camps you Southerners ran in such a brutal manner."

"This is going to get out of hand," Breckinridge said firmly. "Each side will demand more and more of the officers of the other side be handed over to be put on trial. I fear we are on a slippery slope, gentlemen. Each side would be accused by the other of using, to borrow an expression from the California gold miners, kangaroo courts."

"Hasn't there been enough death?" Stephens asked, exasperation and sadness in his voice. "We came here to end a war, yet still seem filled with bloodlust. Can you imagine the outrage that will be generated in the months and years to come, as at least some of these men are found guilty and executed?"

"Mr. Stephens is right," Breckinridge said quickly. "Our task is not only to establish peace, but to create conditions so as to make that peace an enduring one. These tit-for-tat exchanges and demands for people to be handed over by one side to the other side? They will do no good. They will only create more acrimony and bitterness that will make a future conflict between our two nations more likely."

"I don't disagree," Seymour said. "But how can you reconcile that with the need to hold accountable criminals who will otherwise escape justice?"

He thought again of Robertson and felt a familiar feeling of revulsion. "I confess I do not know."

"Perhaps we could set this issue aside for the time being and come back to it later?" Attorney General Black suggested.

Stephens sighed. "There seem to be all too many issues we are setting aside for later."

"That's the truth, by God," Seymour said.

Breckinridge agreed. Not for the first time, he worried that the intractability of both sides was making their task. The possibility of peace was slipping through their fingers.

*   *   *   *   *

The days passed with agonizing slowness. The two sides seemed deadlocked on four issues: the border states, the status of freed slaves, the financial questions of Union reparations versus Southern assumption of the prewar debt, and what to do about officers accused of allowing atrocities. On the first, the Confederates were demanding plebiscites in Tennessee, Maryland, and Kentucky, while the Unionists was steadfastly refusing to consider votes in any of the three states. Exasperated by the Northern intransigence, the Southerners were occasionally threatening to take the possibility of a plebiscite in Louisiana off the table and add a demand for a plebiscite in Missouri or West Virginia, if not both.

There was little movement on any of these questions for a long time. The Confederates were waiting for the Unionists to show some flexibility on Tennessee and Kentucky before dropping their demand for a vote in Maryland, but that moment had yet to arrive.

On slavery, the Confederate delegation, pushed by the iron will of Congressman Miles, was insisting upon a return of the slaves freed by the Union army during the war and refusing to consider the black soldiers taken prisoner as anything but escaped slaves. The Yankees, with former Vice President Hamlin taking the lead, abjectly refused to consider this. A tentative suggestion from Postmaster Reagan that the United States at least compensate the slave owners for their lost property had also been summarily rejected, earning Reagan a reproach from Miles at the delegation's next private dinner. As for a new Fugitive Slave Act, the Yankees merely laughed.

When it was mentioned, the issue of what to do about officers accused of atrocities simply resulted in angry accusations being hurled back and forth across the table. Breckinridge feared this issue almost as much as he did the slavery controversies. It not only threatened to derail the talks altogether, but had the potential to sow the seeds for future conflict if not handled correctly.

The financial questions were not quite as acrimonious as the others, but both sides remained unbending. The Southerners demanded that the United States pay heavy compensation for the damage done by the Union army to civilian property during the war, while the Northerners demanded that the Confederacy assume a substantial portion of the prewar national debt. Neither side seemed willing to give ground.

Some progress was made on miscellaneous technical issues. Breckinridge and Porter had together written a clause for inclusion in the treaty providing for the creation of monuments to the war dead on the various battlefields. The clause stipulated that vandalism or other willful damage to such monuments would be treated by local authorities as a serious crime. Confederate authorities would be prohibited from blocking construction of Union monuments at places like Chickamauga and Fredericksburg, while Union authorities would not be permitted to block construction of Confederate memorials at places like Gettysburg or Wilson's Creek. There was thankfully not much disagreement on this question.

As the days stretched into weeks, Sundays provided the only respite from the endless and increasingly frustrating talks. Breckinridge choose not to attend the religious services at any of Toronto's numerous churches, instead remaining in his room at the Rossin in order to write letters to his wife and clear his mind by reading. He had brought along some of the novels of Sir Walter Scott, which he greatly enjoyed. But these fleeting reading sessions, along with occasional drinks with Colonel Wolseley, were the only escapes Breckinridge was able to gain from the relentless, tedious, and exasperating negotiations.

The Sabbath notwithstanding, the Confederate delegation had decided to have work sessions on Sunday afternoon. Having slept in a bit and gotten some reading done on *Ivanhoe*, Breckinridge had gone to meet his colleagues in their common room at around two o'clock. All of them had been working hard for the past two hours.

"Mr. St. Martin?"

The delegation secretary looked up from his paperwork. "Yes, Mr. Secretary?"

"Colonel Wolseley suggested I try that whiskey made in Scotland. They call it scotch. Could you send down to the bar and see if they have any on hand?"

"Certainly, sir," St. Martin replied. "Are you not enjoying your bourbon, sir?"

"On the contrary, this gift from Captain Weller is superb. But I am beginning to run low, as you can see." He tapped the bottle, the second of the two he had brought to Canada. It was only about a third full. "I want to make sure I find a new supply of ammunition before my present stock is exhausted."

St. Martin chuckled, rose from his seat, and left the room. The other three delegates, ensconced in their own work, said nothing.

Breckinridge returned to reading the map on the table in front of him. It showed Fort Monroe and the nearby rivers and channels. Looking over it, Breckinridge sighed deeply.

"Something wrong?" Reagan asked.

"We cannot allow the Yankees to keep Fort Monroe," Breckinridge said simply.

"Well, we knew that already," Miles replied.

"Yes, but the more I look at this map, the more obvious it becomes."

"How so?"

"Union possession of Fort Monroe would allow them to blockade shipping to and from Richmond and render the naval base at Norfolk useless. But it's worse than that. If the Yankees maintain a sizable army at Fort Monroe as well as one in Washington City, it will allow them to perpetually threaten Richmond from two different directions."

Stephens frowned. "Faced with a constant military threat, we would have to maintain a large army in Virginia even in times of peace. That would be expensive."

"The constant state of danger would also hinder good relations between the Union and ourselves. We would always be suspicious of them."

"That's pretty much what the Yankees said about us, what with Confederate territory in Virginia being right across the Potomac from Washington City. That's why they want the land between the Potomac and the Rappahannock ceded to them."

Breckinridge smiled. "Ah, that's why they brought it up. They want to push us on the land in Virginia."

"Well, we may have to give it to them, then," Miles said sourly. "If what you're saying about Fort Monroe is true, allowing it to remain under Yankee control is intolerable. And we shall definitely need Fort Pickens and the facilities in Key West."

"Need them for what?" Breckinridge asked, confused. It was very unlike Miles to state an opinion on such a technical subject as the location of a military fortification.

"Many of my friends in Congress are looking to the future," Miles said. "Once peace is established with the Yankees and the economy is set in proper order, it shall be high time to look southward. Cuba is anxious to be free from the Spanish yoke, as is well known. It would be best if we might arrange for a peaceful transfer of Cuba from Spain to the Confederacy, but we must be prepared for all eventualities. If the need arises to invade Cuba, Fort Pickens and Key West would be critical bases, wouldn't they?"

Reagan looked at Miles with a disbelieving grin. "Invade Cuba?" The burly Texan chuckled. "I think you're getting a bit ahead of yourself, William. Why don't we finish this peace treaty with the Yankees first?"

"I just want to make sure that nothing gets into this treaty that might hinder the future of the Confederacy," Miles said. "And that future is to be found to the southwards, gentlemen. Cuba first. Then Nicaragua and Honduras. There's almost no limit to what we might achieve. We might even eventually bring Mexico and Brazil into the Confederacy."

98

"William, the Confederacy is in no shape to be embarking on misguided imperial adventures," Breckinridge protested. "Hundreds of thousands of our men were killed winning our freedom. The people are in no mood for another war."

Miles shrugged. "I'm not saying we should make a play for Cuba this year or the next. For all I know, it might take several years before we really get started on this vast project. But we should start thinking about it now."

Breckinridge considered what Miles was proposing to be insane. Trying to gain control of Cuba would surely lead to war with Spain, while any attempt to annex Mexico would just as surely lead to war with France. The government in Richmond was bankrupt and the Southern economy in tatters. Moreover, any military adventures in Latin America would require significant naval power, which the Confederacy noticeably lacked. Miles might as well have suggested launching an attack on the Moon.

Insane or not, Fire-Eaters like Miles had been advocating imperialistic projects in the Caribbean and Latin America for decades. Before the war, the expectation had been that newly acquired territory to the south would eventually be admitted to the Union as slave states. This would mean more Senators and Congressmen defending the institution of slavery, thwarting the plans of the Northern abolitionists to put an end to the institution.

Breckinridge had always considered these schemes unrealistic. But now that the Confederacy had won its independence, the raison d'être for them had vanished. There was no longer any need to defend slavery in the halls of the Senate and House of Representatives, so why did men like Miles remain determined to expand the slave-holding Confederacy to the lands southward?

St. Martin reentered the room, holding a decanter filled with golden brown liquid. Breckinridge smiled as the secretary set it down in front of him.

"You're in luck, sir. The hotel owner said that he had a bottle of scotch on hand, a gift from a regular guest from Scotland."

"Does he not want it for himself?"

"No, sir. The hotel owner is a teetotaler, apparently. He says you are more than welcome to it."

"Well, for once I am delighted to hear that a man is a teetotaler."

He poured himself a glass and carefully took a sip. It did not taste exactly like the bourbons he loved so much, but it certainly was interesting. He made a mental note to thank Colonel Wolseley for recommending it. Breckinridge poured glasses for Miles and Reagan, who gratefully accepted. He did not offer any to Stephens, whom he knew would refuse. It was just as well, for the Vice President's diminutive frame would likely disintegrate from even a small amount of whiskey.

"We need to discuss this issue of trying men for atrocities," Stephens said.

"Yes, we do," Breckinridge agreed. "And I have drawn up a proposal that I think may provide us a way out of our dilemma."

Breckinridge spent the next half hour or so describing his plan, which he had worked on assiduously for the past few days. The other three commissioners listened carefully. Stephens and Reagan occasionally interrupted with questions, but Miles said nothing.

"Very interesting," Stephens said when Breckinridge was finished. "Brilliant, even. I rather wish I thought of it myself."

"Yes, very good work, John," Reagan said. "I think the Yankees will go for it. If they don't, they'll look like hypocrites."

"It is impressive," Miles said. "But I think it may be unnecessary. I expect the Yankees to drop their demand for handing over men accused of atrocities."

Breckinridge's eyes narrowed. "You do? They seem quite adamant on this question."

Miles grinned a slightly sinister grin. "You just wait and see."

Breckinridge felt uncomfortable, as he did so often when Miles spoke. The smile on the South Carolinian's face notwithstanding, his words sounded ominous.

Chapter Four

As they walked up the steps of the York County Court House the next day, July 3, Breckinridge felt optimistic for the first time in weeks. He had high hopes for his plans to resolve the atrocity question. Even better, Stephens had prepared a proposal on the issue of financial reparations and, after some discussion, a decision had been made to offer to cede to the Union three counties in Northern Virginia in exchange for the Union surrendering control of the forts it was claiming in the South. Most of the conference sessions had been exercises in frustrating futility, but Breckinridge today had hopes of making some progress.

"Are you prepared, John?" Stephens asked as they entered the lobby.

"Absolutely," Breckinridge replied with a confidence he did not feel. He knew that the day before him would possibly be among the most important of his life. "I think we've planned things out well enough. With three major proposals to put forward, it is going to be an interesting day, to say the least."

Stephens nodded. "It shall, indeed."

Breakfast passed quickly, with the usual unthreatening banter between the eight men. Concentrating on what he was soon to say regarding the atrocity question, Breckinridge paid little attention to the conversation. Before too long, the dishes were taken away by Edmund and his staff, the coffee was refreshed, and the day's session opened.

"Before we get started, I would like to extend an offer to our Southern friends," Secretary of State Seymour began.

"By all means," Stephens replied, graciously waving his hand over the table to give permission.

"As tomorrow is Independence Day, perhaps we might adjourn the talks early and all meet together for a celebratory dinner? After all, achieving independence from Britain was the collective achievement of both North and South. I see no reason why we cannot celebrate it together."

Breckinridge drew his head back, more surprised than he should have been. Since secession, Confederates had celebrated Independence Day with gusto. After all, many of the leading patriots – George Washington, Thomas Jefferson, and Patrick Henry, among others – had been Southerners. The Confederates might not recall anti-slavery Yankees like John Adams or Benjamin Franklin with the same fondness, but memories of the Revolution remained deeply ingrained throughout the South.

Stephens glanced down the table at his colleagues, wordlessly asking their opinion. A disinterested Miles simply shrugged, while Reagan lazily nodded. Breckinridge decided to speak.

"I think such an occasion might not only be enjoyable, but will help foster good will between the two delegations. Why not celebrate the anniversary of American independence together in the spirit of friendship?"

Seymour smiled. "Good, then. I shall make arrangements and inform you gentlemen of the details this evening, if that is agreeable?"

"It is," Stephens responded.

Breckinridge found the idea delightful. The weeks of talks had stretched the nerves of the delegates to the breaking point. A social gathering might do wonders for everyone's state of mind.

"If I might propose something regarding this dinner?" he said.

"By all means," Seymour replied.

"Might we establish a gentlemen's agreement that no issue currently being discussed in these talks be open for discussion at our dinner? Otherwise, it could simply turn into another session of our conference, albeit with better food and drink."

This comment generated much laughter and Seymour happily gave his assent.

"If we are finished with social planning, might we get down to business?" Miles asked.

"Of course," Seymour said.

The next hour was consumed with more discussion of final borders. As Breckinridge had hoped, some progress on the question was finally made. An agreement was hammered out by which the United States would turn over control of Fort

Monroe, Fort Pickens, and the naval base at Key West to the Confederacy. In exchange, the South agreed to cede land in northern Virginia in order to ensure the defensibility of Washington City. For a time, the Yankees persisted in a demand for all the land between the Potomac and Rappahannock Rivers, but had eventually settled for the counties of Fairfax, Loudon, and Alexandria when the Confederates had threatened to raise a demand for a referendum in Missouri.

"We are in agreement, then?" Stephens asked.

Seymour nodded. "We are."

"Wonderful, wonderful," Breckinridge said with relief. "You see, gentlemen? We can resolve the problems if we work hard enough and maintain mutual trust."

"A good attitude to have, Mr. Secretary," Hamlin answered. "But against the issues of slavery and the border states, these tiny forts and these Virginia counties are small potatoes."

"Speaking of slavery, I have something I wish to discuss," Miles said.

"Very well," Seymour said.

Breckinridge felt a combined feeling of alarm and disgust. Miles had made no mention in the previous day's working session of wanting to bring up anything new regarding slavery. Whatever he was going to say, Breckinridge didn't expect it to be useful.

"I would like to reopen the discussion regarding the slaves carried away by Union forces during the war."

"How refreshing," Hamlin said sarcastically. "We have gone over this issue many times, Congressman. We maintain that those slaves were freed the moment they were liberated by the Union Army, as stipulated by the Emancipation Proclamation. The Confederacy has no ability to counteract this, unless you propose sending men into the United States to capture these people and bring them back to the Confederacy in chains. Attempting to do that, of course, would bring about an immediate resumption of the war."

"Yes, yes, yes," Miles said impatiently. "I know your position. But I wish to ask what I think is a very relevant question. Was the Union Army, in taking away those slaves, acting within the bounds of the United States Constitution?"

Breckinridge frowned. Miles, in constantly bringing up questions of slavery, had become by far the most disruptive person at the conference. Not only were his unrealistic demands taking up time that would have been better spent on other issues, but his constant needling of the Northern delegates was offending them unnecessarily. Breckinridge had tried to talk to Miles about this more than once, but the South Carolinian had always rebuffed him.

Now Miles was trying to bring an entirely new aspect of the question into the picture. Breckinridge remembered the long and fierce debates before the war between Northern and Southern politicians about whether the federal government was empowered by the Constitution to act against slavery in any way. Breckinridge, despite his own qualms about slavery, had always maintained that it was not. A state could choose to abolish slavery within its own borders, but the Constitution did not give the federal government any power to do so.

Miles was still talking. "The United States has maintained, and technically shall continue to maintain until this treaty is ratified, that the Confederate States does not exist as a legal entity and is still part of the United States.

106

Therefore, why do the constitutional provisions protecting slavery where it already exists not apply?"

"I'm neither a politician nor a constitutional scholar," Porter said. "Nor did I support Lincoln's Emancipation Proclamation. But I do know that the Constitution makes the President of the United States the commander-in-chief of the army. The Emancipation Proclamation, as I understand it, was a war measure designed to help defeat the rebellion by removing slaves from Confederate control."

"General Porter is correct," Hamlin said. "President Lincoln explained the proclamation to me at great length when he issued it. Because the use of slaves assisted the Southern war effort, by using them to build fortifications and freeing up white men for military duty, he felt it was within his constitutional authority to free them. Lincoln felt quite strongly, and I agree with him, that he had the legal power to do what he did." Hamlin sighed before going on. "It is a shame that we were not able to free all the slaves."

"I wish to point out that the Emancipation Proclamation was never challenged in the courts," Miles said forcefully. "Its legal status is far from clear. That being the case, I do not see how you gentlemen can be so adamant in your refusal to return the slaves that were stolen from Southerners during the war."

"If the question of the Emancipation Proclamation went before the Supreme Court now, it would be easily upheld," Seymour said. "The majority of the justices were appointed by President Lincoln, including Chief Justice Stanton. I cannot imagine that they would rule the act unconstitutional." Breckinridge thought these words were ironic, since Seymour himself had fiercely opposed Lincoln's appointment of Stanton.

"Perhaps so," Miles replied. "But that doesn't change the fact that the courts have not yet ruled on the question. Constitutionally speaking, therefore, there remains no legal basis for the Union Army to have taken the slaves."

"That's not true," Attorney General Black interjected. "You may not know constitutional law as well as I do, Congressman Miles, but surely you must know that what you're saying is absurd. A court can overturn an executive act or a law passed by the legislature, but the act or law in question remains valid unless and until the court makes such a decision."

"Quite so," Seymour said. "It seems to me that Congressman Miles is bending legal theory to the breaking point in a desperate attempt to find a coherent argument for Southerners to get their slaves back."

"I'm not twisting anything," Miles replied. "I'm merely stating the fact that the courts in the United States have yet to rule on the constitutionality of the Emancipation Proclamation."

Breckinridge noticed something in Miles's tone that he hadn't noticed before. There was an odd hint of calculation in the way Miles spoke. It had been obvious to Breckinridge from the beginning that the Northerners would never give ground on the issues of freed slaves, nor would they countenance any type of new fugitive slave law. Breckinridge had assumed that Miles was either too short-sighted or too ideologically stubborn to realize this. Now, however, he was beginning to suspect that the South Carolinian was up to something else entirely.

Attorney General Black was becoming increasingly irritated. "Even if you were correct, Congressman Miles, it wouldn't matter. Article Six of the United States Constitution specifies that treaties are part of the supreme law of the land.

So if the treaty we are writing here specifies that the slaves freed by the Union Army during the war are, in fact, free, then that shall be their status under the law."

"I acknowledge your right to be mistaken," Miles said, holding up his hands in mock surrender.

"Perhaps we could move on to a more fruitful subject," Stephens suggested. "I believe I have a proposal that might provide us a way out of the impasse regarding financial reparations and the Confederate assumption of prewar debt."

"Very well," Seymour. "Say your say."

Breckinridge listened as Stephens outlined his proposal. The Confederacy would agree to assume one-third of the prewar national debt of the United States, which seemed fair as the Southern states had made up roughly one-third of the prewar population. In exchange, individuals in the Confederacy who had seen their property damaged or destroyed by the Union Army would be given the opportunity to file suit against the federal government. Assuming their cases were successful and the judge ruled that the property damage in question was not militarily justifiable, they would be granted compensation.

"So you're talking about payments to individual citizens," Seymour said when Stephens had finished. "Not direct payments by the United States to the Confederate States."

"Exactly," Stephens replied.

"This proposal has potential," Seymour acknowledged, nodding. "Certainly it will be easier for the Senate to ratify a treaty with a clause such as this, rather than a clause requiring a direct payment to the Confederate government. A direct payment, it has always seemed to me, would imply that the North was the guilty party in the war. This suggestion has much to commend it, don't you think, gentlemen?" He looked at his fellow Northern delegates to gauge their reaction.

Hamlin had raised a finger. "If such a clause is to be included in the treaty, it should be reciprocal," he said firmly. "Northern citizens should have the right to sue the Confederate government for damages caused by the Confederate Army. I'm sure the citizens of Chambersburg would be outraged if Southerners had the privilege of suing Washington for damages, but they did not have the same right to sue Richmond."

"All the people who had their homes in Indiana and Ohio ransacked by Morgan's raiders, too," Black added.

"The particulars can be discussed at length," Stephens said. "Can we agree on this proposal in principle? If so, we can take a great step forward in bringing these talks to a successful conclusion."

"We'll have to discuss it among ourselves before we can give you a commitment one way or the other," Seymour replied. "But I expect that we can find a way to make this proposal work."

Breckinridge felt a profound sense of relief. The knotty financial issue had almost certainly been resolved to the mutual satisfaction of both parties. Granted, of the controversial questions facing the delegates, that of the prewar debt and war reparations was likely to be most easily resolved. Still, the achievement gave Breckinridge confidence that they could tackle the other difficult issues as well. He knew he would need that confidence over the next few minutes.

Stephens glanced at Breckinridge. "And now I believe Secretary Breckinridge has something to say on the atrocity question."

110

"This again?" Porter said unpleasantly. "Last time we discussed it, I grew fearful that Congressman Miles was going to throw his coffee at me."

"I should not like to ruin such an immaculate uniform as yours, General," Miles replied without missing a beat.

The men around the table chuckled. Seymour waited a moment before motioning for Breckinridge to begin.

"The problem with this atrocity question is that each side wishes to punish those officers of the other side who committed crimes while refusing to allow the other side the same liberty with their own officers. My proposal is as follows. A special military tribunal shall be created, including military officers from both armies. Moreover-"

"What good would that do?" Hamlin interrupted. "The two sides would disagree in every case and every vote would be a tie."

"If you would permit me to finish, Mr. Hamlin. The tribunal would also include European officers in an equal number to the total number of Union and Confederate officers. Each side would be bound to respect the findings of the tribunal, whether they agree with them or not."

There was a pause as the Northerners considered Breckinridge's words. He wasn't surprised, for he knew his idea was original. While international arbitration had been used occasionally to resolve border disputes between feuding nations, a tribunal consisting of men of many nationalities such as Breckinridge was proposing was something rather new.

"An interesting idea," Seymour finally said. "I confess I had not thought of that."

Attorney General Black spoke next. "So the thinking is that both our officers and your officers would be permitted to properly defend their own men accused of crimes, while the presence of the European officers would ensure that the voting process of the tribunal would be unbiased."

"That's the general idea, yes."

"Who gets to decide what Europeans get appointed?" Hamlin asked. "I wouldn't want to see the whole tribunal stacked with pro-Confederate officers."

"That's what I was thinking," Seymour said. "We don't trust the British or the French. We'd want the Russians."

"We can work out the specific details later, before writing the treaty clause," Breckinridge said. "My thinking is that both our governments shall extend an invitation to various European countries to send a certain number of officers to participate. Both sides should obviously be allowed to veto the participation of officers they find objectionable. The goal must be the establishment of mutual trust."

"What if the Europeans don't want to participate?" Hamlin asked.

"Why wouldn't they? The Europeans want stability on this side of the ocean and sending a few officers to help the process along costs them nothing."

"The treaty language for this particular clause will be complicated," Black said. "But I must say that I think the proposal itself is very good. Inspired, even. Rather like the recent treaty signed by the European governments in Geneva to ensure that military hospitals are to be considered neutral during times of war."

"Are we in agreement on this, then?" Stephens asked. "If so, I think we can fairly say today's session has been the most fruitful thus far."

Without a word, Seymour turned and looked at his fellow delegates. All nodded.

Breckinridge felt both a sense of relief and a sense of accomplishment. One of the most difficult controversies before the delegates had been resolved and it had been his proposal that had resolved it. More importantly, the tribunal stood a good chance of actually bringing to justice the criminals on both sides who had barbarically murdered wounded men and unarmed prisoners. For just a moment, he felt a sense of hope that Felix Robertson would be one of the men brought before the tribunal to face his own personal judgment day.

"How marvelous," Miles said mischievously. "It will be a lovely thing to see evil men brought to justice. In my opinion, the first person to be brought before this tribunal should be none other than Secretary of War Benjamin Butler, for the murder of Mr. William Mumford in 1862."

Breckinridge's good mood vanished in a flash and he felt a tightening of the stomach. He hadn't thought about the Mumford case in a long time. In 1862, when the armada of Union Admiral David Farragut had run past Confederate river defenses and anchored off New Orleans, several Marines had gone ashore and raised a United States flag over a building. Mumford and several other men had torn the flag down. When Butler, then serving as a general, had led troops into the city nearly a week later, he had had Mumford arrested and, after a quick show trial, hanged. The event sparked outrage across the South and denunciations of Butler around the world. Jefferson Davis had issued an edict that, in the event of his capture, Butler was to be immediately executed.

113

Even thinking about Benjamin Butler was unpleasant, like smelling a fish that had been left on a table for a week. In his entire political career, Breckinridge had never met anyone more corrupt and duplicitous, so utterly devoid of principle, than Butler. A Massachusetts politician, Butler had supported Breckinridge in the 1860 presidential election. When Lincoln had won, Butler had effortlessly shifted from the Democrats to the Republicans, advocating abolitionism and harsh measures against the Confederacy. In 1864, when he concluded that McClellan would win the upcoming election, Butler had had no compunction about going back over to the Democrats. He had worked hard to ensure Lincoln's defeat in the final two months before the election, being later rewarded by President McClellan with the post of Secretary of War.

Breckinridge saw immediately what Miles was doing. Butler's political network was one of the foundations of McClellan's administration. Rather than allowing Butler to be brought before the tribunal, the Northerners would drop the issue of atrocity prosecutions altogether.

"There can be no thought of bringing men of high political office before this tribunal," Seymour said immediately. "Certainly not Secretary Butler."

"Why not?" Miles asked. "He has been accused of murder. Why should he be any different than the others?"

"I think the reasons are obvious to everyone at this table."

"If such a tribunal is set up, the Richmond government will place Butler's name first on its list of those men it wants prosecuted. I'll make sure of that, by God."

Seymour looked at his colleagues uncomfortably. "Well, we shall have to consider our position on this tribunal in a private session before we come to a definitive answer on whether it should be included in the treaty or not."

Miles chuckled slightly. "I thought you might say that."

The elation Breckinridge had experienced a few minutes before turned to gloom. He had worked very hard on his proposal for an independent and objective tribunal and had been very proud of what he had produced. He had even entertained hopes that it might serve as a precedent for future peace treaties between warring powers in Europe. Now Miles had destroyed it, and for no other reason than wanting to protect murderers such as Robertson. It was a disgrace.

Miles had given no hint during the private working session that he intended to do such a thing. Over the course of the conference, Breckinridge had slowly grown to disapprove of and perhaps even dislike Miles. Now, he felt a complete and utter loathing for him.

Stephens saw Breckinridge's discomfort. "I do hope we can salvage something of this tribunal proposal," the Confederate Vice President said. "In the meantime, I believe Mr. Breckinridge has another item to bring up."

"The Secretary of War is outdoing himself today," Seymour said with a smile. "What is this new item, John?"

Breckinridge cleared his throat. He would worry about Miles and the tribunal proposal later. Right now, he had one more important thing to do during this session.

"Gentlemen, the war fueled passions and great anger on both sides. Whatever our final decisions regarding which states shall be in the Confederacy and which in the Union, there will be tens of thousands of men on both sides who will be living in one country while having fought on behalf of the other. Thousands of Missourians and Marylanders fought for the Confederacy, while thousands of Tennesseans fought for the Union. Kentucky men served on both sides as well."

"This is well known to us all, John," Seymour said impatiently. "Might we get to the point?"

"I believe the treaty should include a provision that no official action shall be taken against such men. Union authorities should be prohibited from taking any action against men who served the Confederacy, and vice versa."

"What sort of official actions against these men are you afraid of?" Hamlin asked.

"Prosecution for treason, most specifically," Breckinridge answered. "But beyond that, there are many things to be concerned about. Such people might have their property confiscated, be banned from holding political office, or perhaps even driven from their homes altogether. I think it is incumbent upon us to prevent these things from happening."

"I am not certain," Hamlin replied cautiously. "Under United States law, those individuals did indeed commit treason."

"As Attorney General Black pointed out earlier to Congressman Miles, the treaty we are crafting will have the force of law under our respective constitutions," Breckinridge said. "If the treaty specifies that no one can be prosecuted for fighting on behalf of the other side, then that shall be the law of the land on both sides of the border." Hamlin bowed his head in acknowledgement that Breckinridge was correct.

Miles frowned, which didn't surprise Breckinridge. He, Reagan, and Stephens had not discussed the question with Miles beforehand, assuming that he would not like the proposal. It was well known than Miles and many of his fellow South Carolinians were eager to pass state legislation aimed at those men who had collaborated with Union forces during their occupation of Port Royal on the South Carolina coast. Breckinridge derived just a slight measure of satisfaction at seeing his discomfort.

Black now spoke. "If I recall correctly, did not the Treaty of Paris which ended the Revolutionary War include a provision preventing retaliation against American Loyalists?"

"Yes, it did," Miles said sourly. "It was essentially ignored by the individual states. Most of the Loyalists were forced from their homes and exiled to Canada or the West Indies. And rightly so, if you ask me."

"That was under the Articles of Confederation," Stephens observed. "The central government had no power under those laws to force the states to comply with its wishes. But today the governments in both Richmond and Washington do have the power to enforce such measures as Mr. Breckinridge is proposing. That is, of course, if the two delegations are in agreement?"

"I have no objection," Seymour said. He glanced back and forth at his colleagues, all of whom nodded their assent.

"I am very pleased," Breckinridge said. "As a citizen of one of the states which found itself most divided by the conflict, I think that this provision will do much to heal the wounds of war in both North and South. There has been enough blood spilled and enough hate engendered to last several lifetimes. The restoration of peace between the peoples of the North and South is our universal object here at this conference. Beyond settling the technical issues between our governments, we must always keep in mind the great task of restoring peace and goodwill between our peoples. It's not enough to make peace. We must make a peace that endures."

There was a respectful silence on both sides of the table for a few moments after Breckinridge had finished talking. At first, Breckinridge worried that he had said something objectionable, but quickly realized that the exact opposite was true. He understood that he was a good speaker, which had served him well in his many years as a politician and soldier.

"I'd like to commend the distinguished Confederate Secretary of State," Seymour said. "He has certainly displayed a knack for getting to the heart of the matter."

*   *   *   *   *

It seemed the height of irony that they were celebrating Independence Day in one of the great cities of the British Empire. Then again, Breckinridge had just lived through a war that had torn apart the United States, which he had been brought up to love and revere. He had long since accepted that he lived in a world where ironies abounded.

Secretary of State Seymour had reserved a large room in one of Toronto's finest restaurants for the occasion. In addition to the members of the two delegations, Seymour had invited a dozen or so other Americans who happened to be in the city and, as a courtesy, Mayor Medcalf and some of the prominent members of Toronto society. Rather to Breckinridge's surprise, Mayor Medcalf had happily accepted the invitation and thus far appeared to be the jolliest man in the room. Breckinridge was disappointed that Colonel Wolseley was nowhere to be seen.

As he took his seat, Breckinridge wondered how Seymour had put the event together so quickly. The tableware was exquisite and undoubtedly expensive. Breckinridge didn't know wine nearly as well as he knew whiskey, but he knew enough to recognize excellent Bordeaux when he saw it. The entire room was decorated with draped American flags and other patriotic symbols. Seymour had even had the graciousness to include some Confederate flags.

"Seymour has gone to a lot of trouble, clearly," Stephens said as he slid into the chair next to Breckinridge's. He glanced about nervously at the guests he didn't know, especially the females.

"Indeed," Breckinridge replied. "What do you think Seymour's trying to accomplish?"

Stephens shrugged. "Perhaps he, like us, is tired and frustrated at the slowness of the talks and wanted to use Independence Day as an opportunity for an enjoyable evening."

"You might be right. Still, I suspect there must be some underlying motive for his hosting this dinner."

"I wish I could have found a way to decline," Stephens said. "I would much rather be in my hotel room reading a book."

Breckinridge chuckled. "Cheer up, Aleck. Try to enjoy yourself." He glanced over at Miles, who was sitting a few seats down next to a Connecticut businessman and his wife, a sour expression on his face. "I just hope Congressman Miles doesn't do something to spoil the festivities."

An hour passed as the appetizers and soups were eaten. Several bottles of wine were consumed as well, Breckinridge being very pleased at their quality. The conversation around the table was pleasant and, with the wine glasses being constantly refilled, became increasingly animated. Finally, the main course arrived. Each guest was presented with a plate of beef drenched with a French sauce made from red wine, onions, and shallots, with a selection of roast vegetables on the side. Breckinridge, who was no stranger to good food, thought it one of the most delicious things he had ever eaten.

Another congenial hour passed. To Breckinridge, it seemed as though the guests were talking about every subject imaginable other than the late war or the current negotiations. There was a heated but friendly debate over whether Hector Berlioz or Richard Wagner was the superior composer. The latest book by Charles Dickens was brought up and discussed. The British and Canadian guests seemed obsessed with the question of who Princess Helena and Princess Louise, daughters of Queen Victoria, would marry. The only venture into a political subject was a brief discussion of the rising tensions between Prussia and Austria in Central Europe, which everyone agreed was quite unfortunate.

After listening to the fascinating table talk for some time, Breckinridge realized with some surprise that none of the Southerners were saying anything. Though an educated man, he admitted to himself that he knew little of classical music or most of the other subjects being discussed. Glancing down the table at the other three Confederate delegates, Breckinridge could see in their faces that they felt the same way. Reagan appeared somewhat uncomfortable and bored, while Miles was becoming visibly irritated. Stephens seemed slightly agitated, but Breckinridge put that down to the fact that he was so sensitive in social situations.

From a thousand conversations over the course of his life, Breckinridge knew that his fellow Southerners saw themselves as members of an aristocratic society, infinitely more refined and enlightened than their Northern counterparts. While Southerners enjoyed courtly tea parties on elegant plantations, they imagined their rough Yankee neighbors mindlessly toiling away in sooty factories or warehouses, obsessed as they were with grubby moneymaking. It was an image endlessly described in Southern literature.

Yet how many universities did the South have compared to the North? What was the ratio, North to South, of libraries, theaters, fine restaurants, and the other institutions that formed the basis of a civilized society?

Breckinridge found himself thinking of Thomas Jefferson, one of the great Founding Fathers and a friend and colleague of Breckinridge's own grandfather. Thomas Jefferson was Breckinridge's hero. The man had spoken seven languages, had been an architect and scientist as well as a statesman, and had been able to speak intelligently on any subject being discussed around any dinner table. When was the last time the South had produced such a man as Thomas Jefferson?

For two generations before the war, the rising tensions with the North over slavery had dominated Southern culture. Sitting around the table, listening to the Northern, Canadian, and British guests discussing cultured subjects of which Southerners knew next to nothing, Breckinridge could see the price that the South had paid. For half a century, slavery had eaten away at Southern cultural and intellectual life like a steady dripping of acid. An educated Southerner could discourse for hours on constitutional law or the economics of cotton, but could they hold their own against an educated Northerner or European on subjects of music, art, or philosophy? Breckinridge doubted it, and this fact saddened him.

Having secured its independence, which would soon be formally established by the peace treaty, the South would have to build itself up not just as a nation but as a society. Breckinridge was beginning to realize that it was going to be a much more difficult task than he had ever imagined.

Again, his own internal struggle boiled to the surface. When his tenure as Secretary of War ended, should he retire from public life and resume his law practice or should he seek a new political office? If he choose the former, he would be able to devote himself to his wife and children and perhaps finally cross the Atlantic to see the places he had hitherto seen only in his dreams. But the South needed people like him, Breckinridge knew. People were counting on him to run for Congress, or perhaps even the presidency, and put his talents and energies at the service of the new nation. If he failed to do so, men like Miles would be the ones to decide the destiny of the Confederacy. If Breckinridge retired from public life, would he not be like a general who deserted his own army in the midst of a battle?

Absorbed in these thoughts, Breckinridge almost didn't notice Congressman Miles rise to his feet, wine glass in hand. When he comprehended that Miles had stood to present a toast, Breckinridge instantly became alarmed. The South Carolinian, a hothead under normal circumstances, had already consumed a fair amount of alcohol. Miles tapped his glass with a fork a few times, until the assembled dinner guests quieted. Then he raised his glass.

"I would like to propose a toast to the gallant soldiers of the Confederacy, who fought for four years to secure for themselves those rights that Thomas Jefferson expressed on this day in 1776. Thanks to their sacrifices, the people of the South shall forever enjoy life, liberty, and the pursuit of happiness, in spite of all efforts by the tyrant to hold them under his boot. Against their valor, the rest of the world may struggle in vain."

The room was deathly silent as Miles sipped his wine. Words more calculated to offend their Northern hosts could scarcely have been better chosen. As Miles drank his toast, the other guests remained still in their seats, their wine glasses untouched.

Breckinridge burned with anger. Unlike Miles, who had spent the war as a woman-chasing congressman in Richmond, Breckinridge knew from actual experience how valorous the Confederate soldiers had been. Miles had made the statement in a calculated effort to irritate their Northern counterparts, at a dinner designed to build goodwill between the two sides. He had not only committed a gross violation of etiquette, but had exploited Southern gallantry for his own purposes.

After an awkwardly quiet moment, Hannibal Hamlin rose to his feet.

"I would like to thank the Congressman from South Carolina for his toast and offer one of my own. To the gallant soldiers of the Union, who fought for four years to preserve the great republic created by our Founding Fathers and to free an oppressed people from the chains of slavery."

There was no silence this time. Heartily spoken words of agreement cascaded throughout the room and there was a resounding series of clinks as wine glasses touched one another down the length of the table.

Breckinridge expected Miles to be dismayed by this response. Instead, the South Carolinian did something that Breckinridge did not expect. Rather than glare across the table at the guests who had seemingly humbled him, Miles turned and stared directly at Breckinridge, as if to specifically gauge his reaction to what had just happened. Although he had refrained from actually raising his glass to Hamlin's toast, Breckinridge was still holding it and sipping on the wine. Seeing this, Miles met Breckinridge's eyes. A strange, satisfied smile crossed the lips of the South Carolinian, until he turned again to face Hamlin.

"Do something, John," Stephens whispered.

Neither Miles nor Hamlin had taken their seats. Instead, they simply stared one another down across the table. Breckinridge now rose to his feet to join them. He raised his glass.

"To the gallant men of both armies, Union and Confederate, all of whom fought bravely for what they believed in. And to a firm and lasting peace between the peoples of the North and the South."

The response to Breckinridge's toast was polite rather than enthusiastic, but at least it had not been the embarrassed quiet that had greeted Miles' toast. There seemed a palpable sense of relief as the guests drank to Breckinridge's words. Waiting only a few moments longer, Miles and Hamlin both sat back down.

At that moment, much to Breckinridge's relief, the kitchen staff emerged carrying trays of dessert. One tray was covered in colorful and delicious-looking iced fruits, while another was filled with small dishes of custard garnished with berries. A third tray carried pastries that Breckinridge did not recognize but quickly learned was a French dessert called mille-feuille. Several bottles of champagne were also produced.

The tension of the rival toasts vanished quickly. Within a matter of minutes, happy and animated conversation had resumed around the table. Breckinridge sampled some of the mille-feuille and immediately decided that it was his new favorite dessert. Not only was it delicious in and of itself, but it went perfectly with the champagne.

As the dessert was gradually consumed, the guests began rising from their chairs to mill about the room. Ordinarily, the men would retire to another room for brandy and cigars, leaving the women in the dining room. But there were relatively few women at the dinner, so convention was set aside. Instead, the guests all remained together and more champagne was called for. A string quartet that Seymour had hired entered, quickly set up their instruments, and began playing.

Breckinridge was surprised to see Congressman Miles instantly cast aside his previously harsh countenance and stroll up to Mayor Medcalf with a glass of champagne. The two men were soon locked in what appeared to be a very amiable conversation. Breckinridge was too far away to make out what was being said, but both men were smiling and laughing. It was as though Miles had already forgotten about the incident of the dueling toasts.

As he sipped his champagne, Breckinridge was approached by Vice President Hamlin.

"Might I speak to you for a moment, Mr. Secretary?"

"Of course, Mr. Vice President. I do apologize for Congressman Miles' behavior."

"It was hardly surprising. South Carolinians are raised in a hot climate. It tends to produce hot tempers."

Breckinridge laughed. "That is true."

"But it is not Congressman Miles that I wish to speak to you about. Not directly, anyway."

"Oh?"

Hamlin took Breckinridge by the elbow and guided him away from the table, far enough so that their words could not be overheard by the others. He carefully glanced back at the party guests. Breckinridge noticed that both Seymour and Stephens were eyeing the two of them carefully, obviously curious as to what was being discussed. Miles continued his pleasant conversation with Mayor Medcalf, while Reagan remained in his seat, enjoying a cigar.

"The talks are about to collapse," Hamlin said with conviction.

"I wouldn't be so pessimistic," Breckinridge replied. "I thought we made very good progress at yesterday's session."

"No, you misunderstand me, John. I'm not stating an opinion, but a fact that I can prove to you." Hamlin again glanced back at the party guests. "This is not the place to have this conversation, but it is imperative that you and I speak in private at the earliest opportunity. You must not tell your colleagues about this. May I send word to you as to where to meet?"

"You're asking me to deceive my fellow delegates?" Breckinridge asked, surprised and offended. He cherished his hard-earned reputation for honesty and integrity.

"I apologize if this appears improper. But believe me when I tell you that it is for the good of both our countries. You know and I know that we cannot allow these talks to fail."

Breckinridge stared hard into Hamlin's eyes. The Kentuckian's first thought was that the former Vice President was engaging in a ploy to divide the Confederate delegation. However, he had known Hamlin before the war and, despite their differences, knew him to be an honest man. More importantly, the look in Hamlin's eyes was earnest and pleading. Breckinridge made the decision to trust him, not knowing it was one of the most fateful decisions of his life.

"Very well. Send word to me as to when and where you want to meet. I'll be there."

"Thank you, John."

"But if this is some ploy, Hannibal, I shall make you pay for it."

"It's not."

Hamlin immediately drifted back to the table and picked up another glass of champagne. Breckinridge's mind whirled. What possible explanation could there be for what Hamlin had just told him? What information could he have that would prove the peace talks were about to fall apart? And how could it possibly help for the two of them to secretly meet behind the backs of their respective delegations?

Stephens came up beside him. "What was that all about?"

"Hmm?" Breckinridge asked, distracted.

"What did Hamlin want to talk to you about?"

"Oh. He just asked if there was anything we could do to keep Miles under control."

"Did he?" Stephens asked. "Well, it's not surprising that our South Carolinian friend is getting under the skin of the Yankees, is it?"

"No, not at all," Breckinridge said, forcing a smile. He felt Stephens' eyes examining him, as though searching for any telltale sign of deception. One of the few politician's tricks Breckinridge had never adequately mastered was the ability to lie convincingly. But Stephens simply smiled and said nothing.

*　　　*　　　*　　　*　　　*

The coffee house that Hamlin had chosen was one of many in Toronto and completely nondescript. As Breckinridge sipped a cup of piping hot coffee, he decided that it was the ideal place for a clandestine meeting. Yet he still had no idea what Hamlin wanted to talk about, nor was he comfortable with the circumstances.

"I appreciate you agreeing to meet this like," Hamlin began, sipping on his own cup of coffee.

"I don't see how I could have declined, after what you said," Breckinridge replied. "Having the peace talks fail is not in the Confederacy's interest any more than it is in the Union's. Of course, I am waiting to hear an explanation for all this. I do not like having to deceive my friends, so it had better be a good one."

"Here is the explanation," Hamlin said, withdrawing a paper from his jacket pocket and pushing it across the table. "It is a telegram I received from Senator Sumner."

Mr. Vice President,

I regret the intelligence conveyed in your last message. Let me state emphatically that any treaty which includes provisions returning the freed slaves to a state of servitude, or enacting a fugitive slave law, or failing to release black prisoners in Southern hands, will not be given a hearing in my committee. The same is true of any treaty containing a provision for a secession referendum in Kentucky. If some change in the negotiations does not take place, I shall communicate this fact to the newspapers.

Breckinridge read through the telegram twice more to make sure he understood it. Charles Sumner of Massachusetts was the leader of the Radical Republicans in the Senate and a fervent abolitionist. He had become a household name in 1857 when he had been brutally assaulted on the floor of the Senate by Representative Preston Brooks of South Carolina, an incident which had horrified Breckinridge. He had been one of Breckinridge's staunchest political opponents for many years, but he still respected him as a man of honor and conviction.

As Chairman of the Senate Foreign Relations Committee, Senator Sumner was in a position to scuttle the ratification of the treaty in the Senate, since he could simply refuse to bring it up for consideration in his committee. No doubt the McClellan administration would bring enormous political pressure to bear on Sumner, perhaps by threatening to reduce federal expenditures in Massachusetts and thereby increase unemployment in his state. Yet if any man was willing to stand up to such intimidation, it was Sumner.

The telegram confirmed Breckinridge's greatest fears. Miles' insistence that the treaty contain provisions returning freed slaves to their owners, returning black prisoners to slavery, and enacting a fugitive slave law was about to cause a derailment of the entire peace conference. If Sumner carried through with his threat to publicize what Hamlin had obviously told him about the negotiations, the public furor that would ensue would likely result in both delegations being withdrawn by their respective governments.

Even worse, Sumner was also saying that a referendum to allow Kentucky to join the Confederacy, the most important goal from Breckinridge's personal perspective, was also grounds for an immediate scuttling of the treaty. The whim of a single senator was enough to destroy the dreams of Breckinridge and countless other Kentuckians who had chosen to side with the Confederacy.

If the talks collapsed, what then? In the best case, a nebulous relationship, not quite war but not quite peace, would prevail between the Union and the Confederacy. Investment from Europe would be nonexistent, the government would have to keep thousands of men in the army, inflation would continue to be rampant. The South might be independent, but it would also be on the road to chaos and eventually collapse. In the worst case, war between the North and South would eventually resume, leading to yet more bloody battles with their tragically endless casualty lists.

Breckinridge suddenly realized something else that was obvious. Crumbling the paper in his hands, he glared across the table at Hamlin.

"I thought we had agreed to keep our deliberations secret," he growled.

"Considering the importance of what we are doing, I felt compelled to violate that agreement."

"For all our political disagreements, I have always considered you a gentleman, Hannibal. If a gentleman gives his word, he is expected to keep it."

Hamlin leaned over the table and gripped Breckinridge's hand. "John, I am doing this because I want these talks to succeed. We need a treaty that will be approved by both Richmond and Washington. When that treaty is signed and ratified, feel free to tell every newspaper reporter in the world about what I have done. I won't care then, since I intend to retire home to Maine as soon as we finish our work here."

"And how does leaking secrets to the Chairman of the Foreign Relations Committee, a man who detests the Confederacy, help these talks succeed?"

"Because now you know what the terms must be. Now you know that you must abandon your efforts to get a referendum in Kentucky. Now you know that Miles has to abandon his despicable quest to get these slavery provisions included. Even if we were to acquiesce and include those provisions in the treaty, you now know without any doubt that the Senate will reject it. It won't even get out of committee."

"We've known that all along," Breckinridge said.

"But look at what Sumner is saying, John. He's saying that he'll go to the newspapers unless I can tell him that there's been a change. If he does that, the talks will collapse and there will be no peace treaty."

"Miles won't willingly give up his efforts."

"You'll have to persuade him, then. Or join with Stephens and Reagan to outvote him."

Breckinridge thought again about how Miles had been acting. The South Carolinian was not stupid. In fact, he was a highly intelligent and calculating politician. He had to know that he stood no chance of getting his slavery provisions into the treaty, so why was he pushing so hard for them? Was he so childish that he would risk destroying the negotiations simply to amuse himself? Or did his ideology simply blind him to reality?

He looked up again at Hamlin. "If Senator Sumner specifies these two issues, Kentucky and the slavery provisions, as grounds for killing the treaty ratification, am I to assume that a treaty that does not contain those provisions will be able to get through the Senate?"

Hamlin furrowed his eyebrows. "I cannot say for sure. You and I both know the uncertainty of the legislative process. But if Sumner wants it to pass through his committee, it will do so. At the very least, a treaty without the Kentucky and slavery provisions will get a fair vote on the floor of the Senate."

Breckinridge thought carefully as he took another sip of coffee. He knew how the Senate functioned as well as any man alive, for he had presided over the body for four years as Vice President. In the Democratic electoral landslide of the previous November, the Republicans had seen their majority reduced but not eliminated.

However, if Sumner allowed the treaty to be voted out of committee and sent to the floor for a vote by the full Senate, this would be a tacit admission by the leader of the Radical Republicans that it represented the best deal the Union could get unless they wanted a resumption of the war. Since the Northern people couldn't abide that possibility, the Republicans needed a treaty in order to avoid losing the Senate in the 1866 elections.

His mind whirled. There were so many variables, so many things to take into consideration, that it was as though he were trying to do a complex algebraic equation in his head. If the treaty went too far in favor of the Confederacy, Sumner would make sure that it died in committee. But if it was seen as too harsh on the Confederacy, giving them nothing beyond their independence, than Miles might encourage his fellow Fire-Eaters to block its ratification in Richmond.

There was also the reaction of the public to take into account. Even if the slavery provisions so dear to Miles were included in the treaty, and even if Sumner then allowed the treaty to pass through his committee and be approved by the Senate, the reaction in abolitionist strongholds like Boston would be terrible to behold. There would be riots in the streets. Relations between North and South would be poisoned even more deeply than they already were.

"If the Confederacy does acquiesce in the freedom of these slaves, what shall become of them?" Breckinridge asked. "They cannot remain in the South, you know."

"Yes, that is clear," Hamlin replied. "They'd just be returned to slavery sooner or later, no matter what the treaty says. You may be a man of honor, John, but when it comes to slaves, there are relatively few men of honor in the Confederacy."

"So they shall go to the United States?"

"There is no alternative."

"But we're talking about hundreds of thousands of people."

Hamlin shrugged. "Shiploads of European immigrants arrive in Boston and New York every day. The North is used to bringing in newcomers. We'll manage."

Breckinridge thought Hamlin was being entirely too optimistic. Workers in the industrial towns, native and immigrant alike, would see the freed slaves as competitors for jobs, pouring fuel onto the fire of racial prejudice. It would be an ideal situation for political demagogues to exploit for their own advantage. In any case, it would be a problem for the North to deal with.

133

"If I am to get Miles to drop his insistence on the slavery provisions, what can I give him in return?" Breckinridge asked.

Hamlin sat back in his chair. "I expected that you would ask this. What if you and I work together to include some economic provisions in the treaty that would benefit South Carolina in particular?"

"What sort of provisions?"

"South Carolina's economy is dependent on exports of cotton, sugar, rice and tobacco. The economies of all the Southern states are export-driven, of course, but South Carolina is more so than the others. We could include a provision specifying that the Confederacy is to be granted most-favored-nation status as far as trade with the United States is concerned."

Breckinridge nodded. "So our exports to the Union won't be subject to any high tariffs or other trade barriers?"

"Exactly. No higher than we impose on the imports of raw materials from other countries, anyway. And since the United States has no cotton or tobacco of its own, we can't afford to enact a high tariff on those particular commodities anyway."

Breckinridge thought for a moment, nodding. "Yes, that would please a great many people in the South. Wealthy plantation owners in particular."

"It will upset many people in the North, no doubt. There are many who want to punish you, just as Britain punished America after the Revolution by stopping us from trading in the Caribbean. But if that's the price to get Miles to

134

stop pushing for those slavery provisions, thereby giving the treaty at least a chance of ratification, I am willing to pay it."

"It is a good provision anyway. I've always favored free trade and opposed protectionism."

"So have most of you Southerners. It is not so with us in the North, as you know. So including such a provision represents a significant concession from our side, as I hope you appreciate."

"I do, I do," Breckinridge said quickly. "But this would be about more than helping the economy of South Carolina. Trade between our two countries would go a long way to preserving peace. And that is something we must keep in mind, you and I. We may succeed in establishing peace here, but we must also focus on doing it in such a way as to make it unlikely for war to ever break out again in the future. If we don't, it would be like Britain and France in the eighteenth century, with peace treaties being nothing more than temporary truces between wars."

Hamlin shook his head. "It will take generations before the bitterness created by this war fades away."

"Perhaps so. But reestablishing commercial ties will help that process. If Northern factories are still fed by Southern cotton and Southern farmers still purchase Northern manufactured goods, it may give pause to leaders in either Richmond or Washington who might otherwise contemplate war."

"The cotton you speak of will be grown by the labor of enslaved Africans," Hamlin said pointedly. "The treaty may encourage trade between our two countries, but many a Northern factory owner may choose to buy his cotton elsewhere."

"Well, there's nothing to be done about that. The government can't force a factory owner to buy cotton he doesn't want to buy."

Hamlin waited a moment before going on. "How do you wish to proceed now?"

"Let me talk with Stephens and Reagan about all this before we discuss it with the full delegation. If the three of us can present a united front against Miles on the slavery provisions, we can overcome his objections."

Hamlin looked carefully at Breckinridge. "And Kentucky?"

Breckinridge pursed his lips beneath his whiskers and shook his head. "It's a bitter pill to swallow, Hannibal. I don't mind telling you. It means living the rest of my life as an exile from my own land. And not just me. Men like John Morgan, Simon Buckner, and all the thousands of soldiers who served in the ranks of the Orphan Brigade. They served honorably and endured great hardships for the South."

"They can return to Kentucky if they so wish. We've already agreed to include provisions preventing retaliation against men who served on the other side, haven't we?"

"Well, there's the letter of the law and then there's reality, isn't there?"

"True enough. But as I've made clear, giving up the referendum in Kentucky is necessary to get the treaty through the Senate. To put it bluntly, John, you have no choice."

"I know." Breckinridge paused a moment. "You will have to give in on Tennessee, though."

"And we are prepared to do that. Seymour and the others have already said as much as to me. As long as you drop all claims to Kentucky, Missouri, Maryland, and West Virginia, we will allow a referendum in Tennessee."

"So, just to be clear. If my delegation gives up the slavery provisions being pushed by Congressman Miles, your delegation will include a provision granting most-favored-nation trade status to the Confederacy. And if we give up the referendum in Kentucky and the other border states, you will grant the referendum for Tennessee. Is this correct?"

Hamlin nodded. "Completely correct."

"What about the military tribunal for those accused of atrocities?"

Hamlin shook his head. "We received a wire from President McClellan. The tribunal is a deal-breaker. The President cannot accept the possibility of Secretary Butler being put on trial."

"So the atrocity question is completely dropped?"

"That's right."

Breckinridge frowned as he nodded. "I thought as much. Damn that Miles."

"For what it's worth, John, I thought your concept of an international tribunal was a dazzling one. When this is all over, I suggest you write it up and have Judah Benjamin circulate it through the capitals of Europe. It may do some good."

"I'll think on that later, when I'm back in Richmond."

"Very well. As for now, so long as you and I understand one another, I think we have an agreement."

"Yes, I think so, too."

Hamlin reached his hand across the table. Breckinridge firmly shook it.

Chapter Five

"I don't like it," Miles said firmly. "I don't like it and I cannot understand why you do not agree with me."

"But the Yankees will not agree to the treaty otherwise," Stephens protested. "And including a provision that grants the Confederacy most-favored-nation status will be of great benefit to the economy of your state. It's a big concession by the Yankees, you must acknowledge."

"I'm delighted that the Yankees are willing to include a clause on trade," Miles said. "But I do not see why they remain opposed to the three slavery provisions I have outlined. They seem entirely fair to me."

Breckinridge sat quietly, listening while Stephens tried to wear Miles down. The conversation had been going on for over an hour. Miles was rehashing the same points over and over again, just as he had done from their first conversation on the subject when they had been standing near the bow of the

CSS Shenandoah. But Breckinridge could tell that he was wearying of the contest and was now fighting a rear guard action merely to save face. The combined persuasive power of Breckinridge, Stephens, and Reagan was winning the battle by sheer attrition.

Things were unfolding better than Breckinridge had hoped. As he had promised Hamlin, Breckinridge had quietly approached both Stephens and Reagan outside of the regular daily delegation meeting. Without entirely revealing how he knew, Breckinridge had persuaded them that Miles had to stop pushing the slavery provisions immediately. They had both appeared skeptical at first, but Breckinridge's willingness to give up on the Kentucky referendum had demonstrated his earnestness. They didn't ask how he knew what he knew; they simply trusted him.

"Well, if I cannot have the slavery provisions, fair and right though I think them to be, then I suppose I can be persuaded to accept this favorable trade provision," Miles said. "I would rather take something from these talks than nothing. Common sense, yes?"

"Indeed," Breckinridge said with firmness. "Common sense."

"Well, that's it, then," Miles said, sighing heavily. "I have fought this fight with all my strength, but I now must concede defeat. I think we shall pay a great price, though. The escaped slaves represent massive financial losses to plantation owners across the Confederacy. And without a fugitive slave provision, we shall face a never-ending stream of runaways trying to escape into the Union."

"Issues for another time," Stephens said. "We need to get this treaty signed and bring these talks to a successful conclusion. Once that is done, and the treaty is ratified by the respective Senates, we can begin worrying about the aftermath."

Miles chuckled bitterly. "Say that if you like, but I shall begin worrying about it now." He looked over at Breckinridge. "And you, John! I'm surprised to hear that you have caved into the Yankee demands and given up on the Kentucky plebiscite."

"We have to face facts, William," Breckinridge responded. "If we insist on a Kentucky plebiscite, the Northern delegation will depart Toronto without a treaty being completed. That would be a disaster. By giving it up, we gain what we want with regard to Tennessee and, more importantly, a treaty that can pass muster with the Senate in Washington."

"You're happy to live out the rest of your life as a permanent exile from the land of your birth?" Miles taunted, "The land where your family has lived for generations?"

"No, I'm not," Breckinridge said firmly. "But I am willing to face up to reality, no matter how unpleasant it may be."

"These freed slaves cannot remain in the Confederacy," Miles said firmly. "On that question I shall not be moved."

"I agree," Breckinridge said. "We shall require that the clause applies only to those slaves that have relocated to the North."

"Virtually all of them, in other words?"

"That's correct."

Miles shrugged. Breckinridge thought that his capitulation had been rather too easy and suspected that the resistance Miles had put up had been done mostly for show. Clearly the South Carolina congressman had long before accepted that he wouldn't get his cherished slavery provisions. Breckinridge was beginning to wonder if he had, in fact, ever been serious about them. What game had the man been playing?

Reagan cleared his throat. "So, we're in agreement, then? We agree to drop our demand for the slavery provisions in exchange for a trade clause that benefits us, and we agree to drop the demand for a referendum in Kentucky and the other border states in exchange for one in Tennessee?"

Breckinridge and Stephens both immediately voiced their assent. All eyes turned on Miles, who sat in his chair with his arms folded, looking to Breckinridge like nothing so much as a petulant child.

"I suppose it doesn't much matter," Miles finally said. "Simply by establishing the independence of the Confederacy as a white-ruled, slave-based nation, we have achieved our great purpose. Liberty, after all, is an acquired privilege, not a natural right. We've freed ourselves from the Yankees and their dangerous notions of egalitarianism. We've freed ourselves from the monstrous and dangerous fallacy of Thomas Jefferson, who wrongly asserted that all men are created equal. Against that, whatever we're giving away in this treaty will count for little in the long run."

Breckinridge felt it would be wise to hold his tongue, but could not. "We did not establish the Confederacy on the principle of slavery, William. We did it simply to be free to work out our own national destiny on our own terms. And as for the conviction of Thomas Jefferson that all men are created equal, I shall always be proud of the fact that my great-grandfather was one of the men who affixed his signature to the Declaration of Independence."

Miles waved his hand dismissively. "We'll wait for history to judge us, John. The Confederacy, you see, is a great experiment. Our nation will be a beacon for the world, upholding the principles of aristocracy and slavery. Let the Yankees muck about with equality, abolitionism, and democracy, if they choose. In the meantime, our Confederacy shall expand southwards. Cuba, Nicaragua, Mexico and eventually Brazil. I'll swallow the disappointments of this treaty, my friends, because in the long run they shall be nothing but temporary setbacks. The future, if you ask me, is bright."

Breckinridge listened to Miles's monologue with increasing dismay. He knew that Miles's vision for the future of the Confederacy was shared by many powerful men in the South. It was not a vision that Breckinridge shared. He asked himself again whether he had to be the man to stop it.

*   *   *   *   *

Breckinridge went into the negotiating session of July 12 with higher expectations than he had felt since the talks had begun more than a month before. He was certain that they were about to come to the climactic moment of the conference. Having made a deal with Hamlin at their secret meeting, and having gotten the rest of his own delegation on board, Breckinridge could now only pray that Seymour and the rest of the Northerners would agree to the terms.

As the Southerners strode through the entrance hall of the York County Court House, Miles came up beside Breckinridge.

"I do hope Edmund's coffee service is good this morning," Miles said matter-of-factly.

"The coffee has been good every other morning," Breckinridge replied. "I see no reason for today to be any different."

"Well, you know all about good coffee. Don't you, John?"

Breckinridge didn't turn to look at Miles, instead continuing to stare straight ahead. Miles nonchalantly walked up beside Reagan and politely asked him how his morning was going. Stephens, oblivious to the entire conversation, simply continuing walking down the hall, absorbed in his own thoughts.

Breckinridge's breathing quickened. Had what Miles said been meaningless banter or did it mean that Miles knew about his secret meeting with Hamlin? If it was the latter, how could he possibly have found out?

Breckinridge told himself that he was being paranoid and quickly pushed Miles's words from his mind. Perhaps he was feeling guilty for having gone behind the backs of his colleagues. Had he not met with Hamlin, such a comment as the one Miles had just made would not have raised any concern. He couldn't allow such silly thoughts to distract him from what was going to be the most important day of the deliberations.

The delegation entered the meeting room. For once, the Union representatives had arrived first and had already begun eating their breakfast. After so many negotiating sessions, an

144

unspoken agreement had developed that everyone should simply start eating when they arrived, etiquette be damned. They had all gotten to know one another quite well over the past several weeks and no one was likely to take offense at this.

"Good morning, gentlemen," Seymour said with genuine warmth, standing from his chair and extending his hand across the table. The now habitual handshakes were exchanged by all present.

The breakfast, consisting of bread, bacon, eggs, and fried mushrooms, passed quickly. Edmund's staff cleared away the dishes and brought in another coffee service before quietly departing, leaving the Americans alone.

"Well, shall we begin?" Stephens asked affably.

"By all means," Seymour said.

Stephens glanced at his fellow Southerners for one final moment of reassurance before looking back across the table. "We are willing to make an offer on the issue of plebiscites in Kentucky and Tennessee."

"An offer, eh?" Attorney General Black said with a hint of sarcasm. "I hope it's a good one, as we've been talking past one another on those questions since the first day of these talks."

"We have, indeed," Stephens said. "We have been insisting that referendums be held in both states to allow them to decide whether to remain in the Union or join the Confederacy. You have been equally adamant that neither state be allowed such a vote and that both remain within the Union."

"So what is your offer, then?" Seymour asked.

Stephens cleared his throat and sat up in his seat. "We are willing to drop our demand for a plebiscite in Kentucky if you, in return, agree to such a vote in Tennessee."

"That sounds reasonable to me," Seymour said instantly and nonchalantly. He glanced at his colleagues. "Gentlemen?"

Porter unenthusiastically nodded his head, while Black muttered that he agreed. It was immediately obvious to Breckinridge that the Northerners had decided ahead of time that they would follow this course of action.

"I have no objection," Hamlin said. "Of course, the treaty provision must include stipulations to ensure that the vote in Tennessee is free and fair."

"Of course," Stephens said.

Porter, a frown on his face, broke in. "If we are to agree to this, there should also be a clause in the treaty that says that the Confederacy drops all claim to the other disputed territory. Maryland, Missouri, West Virginia, and New Mexico, I mean."

"We've already agreed to that, in principle," Miles said. "If the treaty doesn't specify that we maintain a claim to it, isn't that enough?"

"No," Porter said firmly. "I think it needs to be specified."

Breckinridge was surprised to hear General Porter's words, as he had generally refrained from speaking on subjects not directly related to military matters. But he had to concede that Porter's point was a good one.

"If the Confederacy is sincere in surrendering its claims to the border states, why would you object to including such a provision in the treaty?" Seymour asked.

"Because it is unnecessary," Miles retorted.

"Even if you are correct, what difference does that make?" Porter said angrily. "Are you afraid we will use too much paper?"

"Let us remain calm, gentlemen," Breckinridge said earnestly. "We're making good progress this morning."

"Despite what Congressman Miles says, I think such a provision is very necessary," Hamlin interjected. "We are establishing peace with this treaty, but we must also take care to ensure that the peace lasts. If the treaty does not specify that the Confederacy abandons its claims to all the border states, their status will remain a sore point in relations between our two countries. It could potentially lead to conflict in the future."

Breckinridge nodded. "I agree with Mr. Hamlin. If we are sincere in limiting our claims to Tennessee, there is no honorable reason for us to reject a provision on this point in the treaty. Otherwise, the Confederate representatives from Kentucky and Missouri will continue to sit in the Confederate Congress and the Confederate governors of those states will maintain administrations-in-exile on Confederate territory. Not an ideal situation, to say the least. It would be best for all concerned to nail down precisely the status of the disputed states."

"I'm inclined to agree with Secretary Breckinridge," Stephens said firmly, looking sternly at Miles. The South Carolinian simply shrugged and said nothing in response.

"I can have the relevant text ready tomorrow morning for everyone's perusal, if that is agreeable," Black said. "Two articles. One for the referendum in Tennessee and one stating that the Confederacy gives up its claims to the other border states."

"Completely agreeable to our side," Stephens said.

Seymour exhaled sharply. "Well, I must say that I am very glad to get that out of the way. The issue of borders has given me more headaches than anything else since the beginning of these negotiations."

"And myself as well," Breckinridge said. "Having come to an agreement on the border states, I think I can honestly say we're close to completing these negotiations."

"Perhaps," Hamlin said carefully. "The only major obstacle that remains now, it seems to me, is the insistence of the Confederate delegation on certain provisions related to slavery. I refer specifically to the demands for a return of slaves freed under the Emancipation Proclamation, the enslavement of black prisoners of war, and requiring the United States to return to the Confederacy slaves which escape into its territory."

Black grunted. "This remains difficult ground. You Southerners have been distinctly unwilling to compromise on these matters thus far."

Breckinridge was not surprised to see the eyes of the Northerners fall on Miles. The South Carolina congressman sat silently, meeting the gazes of the men on the other side of table with a smug grin.

"We are prepared to make a new offer on that question as well," Stephens said calmly.

Seymour drew his head back in surprise. "Are you?"

"Yes, we are," Stephens replied. "We are willing to abandon our efforts on these clauses. In fact, we are willing to have provisions included in the treaty that specify freed slaves are not to be returned and black prisoners are to be treated no differently than whites. In exchange, we would like the treaty to include clauses guaranteeing most-favored-nation trading status between the Union and Confederacy."

Porter's eyes narrowed. "Most-favored-nation status?" It was obvious from the Union general's tone that he did not know what the phrase meant.

Attorney General Black sensed Porter's confusion and responded. "It's a term in international law, General Porter. Essentially, it would mean that the United States could not impose trade barriers such as tariffs on the Confederacy that are any higher than the those we impose on the country with whom we have the lowest tariff. Does that make sense?"

"No," Porter admitted.

Black thought for a moment and then spoke again. "Suppose the lowest import duty the United States imposes on cotton imports is a ten percent import duty on cotton imported from Brazil. If we were to grant the Confederacy most-favored-nation status, we could not impose a tariff on cotton from the Confederacy any higher than ten percent. And if we then lowered the tariff for Brazil, we would have to lower it for the Confederacy as well."

Porter grunted. Breckinridge wasn't sure if he still didn't understand or if he simply did not care about something so esoteric. Breckinridge knew from long experience that it was far more than a mere technical matter. If the Confederacy were granted most-favored-nation status with the United States, it would be of enormous economic benefit to the country. Southerners of every stripe, from poor farmers to the owners of large plantations, had been economically ruined by the war. The South would need to be able to begin exporting large amounts of cotton and tobacco to foreign markets as quickly as possible in order to bring in hard cash and begin to repair the economy. Obtaining most-favored-nation status from the United States, thereby reopening the vast Northern market to Southern exports, would be a huge step forward.

"There will be resistance to this in the North," Seymour pointed out. "Especially in New England. Some will want to put tariffs in place to hinder the sale of cotton grown by slaves."

"Perhaps so," Breckinridge said. "But it will also increase employment in Northern factories. With so many veterans coming back from the war, and with military contracts drying up, lots of men are going to be looking for work. Economically speaking, low tariffs on imports of raw materials help the Union as much as they do the Confederacy."

"True," Seymour said. "I'll have to make that argument to the senators from New England when the time comes. They're idealists, as you know, but they also want their constituents to have jobs."

"So you agree to our proposal?" Stephens asked hopefully.

Seymour nodded. "We have no objection. We wouldn't ordinarily want to include a provision for most-favored-nation status in the treaty, but if it is the price to pay for getting you to drop your slavery provisions, so be it."

Breckinridge noted that Seymour had made the decision without asking the opinion of his colleagues and that none of them had objected. He also noticed a slight but satisfied grin on Hamlin's face. Putting those two observations together, Breckinridge concluded that Hamlin had persuaded the rest of his delegation to go along with the idea ahead of time, just as he had with the provisions about Tennessee and Kentucky. Porter's confusion seemed to indicate that he had not been part of the discussions. What this hinted about the internal workings of the Union delegation, Breckinridge couldn't guess.

Seymour sat back in his chair, smiling broadly. "Well, it seems that we have accomplished more in the last hour than we have achieved in several weeks of negotiations."

Stephens chuckled. "It's astonishing what men can accomplish when they choose to be reasonable."

Hamlin frowned and shifted uncomfortably. "Had the South chosen to be reasonable after Lincoln won the 1860 election, rather than pull the country down into the nightmare of civil war, none of this would have been necessary."

"That's enough of that," Seymour snapped at his fellow delegate. "What's done is done. With the concessions each side has just made, we have the framework for a workable treaty. Let us leave the bickering to the historians."

"The historians will bicker, no doubt," Porter said. "We generals and politicians will certainly give them ammunition enough when we write our memoirs."

This comment generated a round of laughter around the table. Breckinridge wondered how many of the men in the room were already getting ready to put pen to paper as soon as they returned home.

The two delegations decided that Attorney General Black and Postmaster Reagan would together write the specific text of the treaty, incorporating the various decisions and compromises that had been hammered out over the previous few weeks. Once this was completed, the two delegations would again meet and make any final corrections or amendments.

"And then?" Breckinridge asked.

"And then our task shall be done," Seymour replied.

*   *   *   *   *

"Five thousand?" Breckinridge asked. "That's all?"

"A bit less than that, actually," Wolseley answered. "Maybe forty-eight hundred? The French had about the same number, but less than half of them were regulars. Most of them were militia, not well-armed or well-trained."

"Interesting that a battle of such momentous historical consequence was fought by so few men," Breckinridge mused.

Breckinridge thought that the Plains of Abraham, the field outside Quebec where the great battle had been fought more than a century before, was quite beautiful. The rolling hills of green grass, the ancient trees that swayed gently in the breeze, and the sharp bluffs overlooking the vast St. Lawrence River combined to give the scene a grand and majestic quality. It seemed an appropriate setting for an epic battle.

Colonel Wolseley was proving himself to be an excellent tour guide. Pointing and gesturing as they walked the field, he told the story of the engagement with a knowledge clearly gleaned from extensive study and multiple trips to the battlefield. He described to Breckinridge the actions of the various regiments of British regulars, Scottish Highlanders, and American volunteers, as well as the opposing French units. He described the heroics of the two opposing commanders, James Wolfe for the British and Louis-Joseph de Montcalm for the French, both of whom had been mortally wounded during the terrible fighting.

The excursion had thus far been a tonic for Breckinridge. When Black and Reagan had reported that it would take at least three days to complete the task of preparing the text of the treaty, giving the other delegates some unexpected free time, Breckinridge had immediately sought out Wolseley to take him up on the offer to visit Quebec. During the train journey northeast, his conversations with Wolseley about military history, the respective merits of bourbon and scotch, and various other subjects had eased much of the pressure Breckinridge had felt over the past several weeks. He knew that he would at least take home from Toronto the fact that he had made a new friend.

"The battle wasn't the end of the war, of course," Wolseley was saying. "In fact, the French tried to recapture Quebec the following year, in 1760. They managed to win a tactical victory outside the walls of the city, but were unable to retake Quebec itself."

"I had never heard that," Breckinridge replied, fascinated.

"It's not talked about much," Wolseley said. "You and I read historians who write in English, obviously. They're only human, and tend to dwell on those events in which their side won rather than those in which it lost. But in that particular case, the momentary success of the French gained them nothing. It certainly couldn't undo Wolfe's great achievement."

"And it was a great achievement," Breckinridge said. "By capturing Quebec, Wolfe basically destroyed the French empire in the Americas. Whatever else happened, he made certain that the people who inhabited North America spoke English rather than French."

"Yes, indeed. It could have all remained part of the British Empire, had not your forefathers gotten so upset about that silly tax dispute. Or perhaps if Burgoyne had not been so foolish at Saratoga."

Wolseley chuckled at his own joke, but Breckinridge thought he had detected a very slight trace of bitterness in the colonel's words. Breckinridge almost found it amusing that the memory of the American Revolution could still upset an Englishman after nearly a century had passed. If they still had any reason to be upset about losing America, he mused to himself, the British conquest of much of the rest of the world should have gone some way to compensate them.

His mind continued wandering down this line of thought. How long, Breckinridge wondered, would there be bitterness between Northerners and Southerners on account of the War for Southern Independence? Would there ever come a day when men from the two countries could tour the battlefields at Gettysburg or Chickamauga together and discuss what had happened there without animosity?

There had been no open conflict between Britain and America since the War of 1812. There had been tensions, to be sure, but overall relations between the two countries had been proper and trade between them had flourished. Might the Union and the Confederacy one day enjoy a similar relationship? Breckinridge prayed it would be so. The treaty he had just played so critical a role in crafting would hopefully begin a process of reconciliation.

They continued strolling across the battlefield. Wolseley occasionally pointed to certain spots and described what a particular unit had done there. Eventually, Wolseley came to a halt.

"We are now standing on the spot where Wolfe was shot."

"Right here?" Breckinridge asked in surprise, looking down at the ground.

"Near as we can tell," Wolseley replied. "He was hit three times in rapid succession. The third bullet struck him in his chest and it proved to be mortal."

"Shots to the chest usually are," Breckinridge said. He knew this from experience, having seen far too many men die agonizing deaths from such wounds.

"Wolfe lived long enough to be told that the French lines had broken and the enemy was retreating. He knew he had won the victory."

"I suppose that's something," Breckinridge replied.

"The last words he spoke, according to the witnesses, were `I die contented.'"

Breckinridge doubted that very much, but tactfully declined to say so. For just a moment, he remembered kneeling beside his mortally wounded friend Robert Hanson, his successor as commander of the Orphan Brigade, during the attack on the final day of the Battle of Murfreesboro. Hanson had not been able to die contented like Wolfe, however, for the attack he had been leading had been bloodily repulsed.

"What better way to die than to die for one's country?" Wolseley asked. "To be honest, I rather envy Wolfe."

"I'd rather live for my country than die for it," Breckinridge replied.

Now Breckinridge couldn't shake the memory of the last day at Murfreesboro. The Orphan Brigade, his beloved unit which had been attached to his division that day, had gone into the attack with twelve hundred men and come out with scarcely half that number. The men had placed their faith in him when they had elected to fight for the South even though their state remained in the Union. Because of the stupidity of Braxton Bragg, hundreds of them had perished. The brigade had been utterly cut to pieces.

"To each their own," Wolseley said. "As I have said to you before, I am but a soldier. Beyond knowing that I am doing my duty for queen and country, I wish to be remembered by my fellow soldiers. What better way for me to achieve that than to die in battle? Now you, on the other hand, have another option. You're neither soldier nor statesman, but one of those curious hybrids that blends elements of both into a single man. I don't know how you do it, but you do. So you, unlike me, get to choose."

"Choose what?"

"Choose how you want to be remembered. You have been a good soldier, John. Your victory at New Market will be remembered as long as men study war. You fought well in many different battles. You took care of your men and acted in a gallant manner towards your foes. But your story is not yet over. You're how old?"

"Forty-four."

"Quite so. You have decades left. While I'm seeking glory on some battlefield in some godforsaken corner of the world, you can be doing something more for your new country. Something that doesn't involve being a soldier."

Breckinridge's mind whirled. The carnage he had seen at Murfreesboro had been bloody, indeed, but it had been only one battle among many. He remembered Shiloh, Chickamauga, Monocacy, and Third Winchester. As far as William Poacher Miles and his Fire-Eater friends were concerned, the Southern boys who had died upon those fields had given their lives to create a Confederacy in which a small and wealthy elite, who made their fortunes from the labor of slaves, would lord it over all those they considered their inferiors. The latter category would include whites as well as blacks. Indeed, it would include the soldiers that Breckinridge and his fellow generals had led during the war.

He thought of his wife Mary, patiently waiting for him back at their house in Richmond with their children. The war had necessarily caused them to spend years apart from one another. Settling down to a legal practice in Richmond, or perhaps Atlanta or New Orleans, would give him time to enjoy his marriage in a way he never had before. The new nation would certainly offer various business opportunities as well.

Yet if Breckinridge did decide to leave public life, would he not be abandoning his duty? Congressman Miles was far from the only radical Fire-Eater eager to take the Confederacy down a dangerous path of imperialism and confrontation. If the forces of moderation and common sense did not rally to oppose them, such men would soon win a majority in the Confederate Congress. When the presidential election came in 1867, one of them might be elevated to the highest office in the land.

There was something else, too. As these thoughts rolled through his mind, Breckinridge felt the familiar pull of ambition and desire for renown that had first been ignited within him when he had been a young boy reading the stories of the ancient Greek and Roman heroes. If he stepped out of public life now, he would be remembered as an unremarkable vice president, a failed presidential candidate, and a somewhat successful general, if he were to be remembered at all.

He recalled a quote from Napoleon.

Everything on earth is soon forgotten, except the opinion we leave imprinted upon history.

He made a decision in that moment. In 1867, he would run for President of the Confederate States of America.

"Shall we continue the tour?" Wolseley asked, his friendly tone flavored with a hint of curiosity.

"I'm sorry?" Breckinridge replied. He belatedly realized that several awkward minutes had passed in silence as he had wrestled with his emotions.

"There is still more to see on the battlefield. And perhaps then we could find a place in town to have a drink."

"Yes, yes, of course," Breckinridge stammered.

"You seemed lost in thought there for a few minutes, my friend."

"I was," Breckinridge admitted. "I hope I was not being rude."

"Far from it, General. I would be interested to know what you were thinking about."

Breckinridge chuckled. "And I would tell you, Colonel, but my wife would be angry if she were not the first person to know."

*　　　*　　　*　　　*　　　*

Breckinridge's hand almost trembled as he held the pen. He leaned over the table, signing his name first to the Union copy, then the Confederate copy. He was terrified that the pen might slip in his hand, blotting the ink and ruining the appearance of his signature. Part of his nervousness was due to the presence of dozens of people lining the walls, local notables or visiting Americans who had crowded into the room to watch the ceremony. To his great relief, his hand remained steady and his signature was perfectly legible.

Seymour and Stephens, as the heads of the respective delegations, had affixed their signatures first. A coin toss overseen by Mayor Medcalf had given Stephens the right to go before Seymour. This had caused a wry comment from General Porter about how luck always seemed to favor the Confederacy, which had brought forth a bit of laughter from all save Vice President Hamlin.

One by one, the remaining commissioners stepped forward to sign the two copies of the treaty. Each kept their pen as a keepsake. The actual signing of the treaty took less than five minutes.

Seymour motioned for Edmund the valet, who stepped forward with a tray of champagne flutes. Each of the eight commissioners took one.

"Gentlemen," Seymour said grandly. "To peace!"

"To peace!" the eight commissioners said as one as they clinked their champagne flutes together. The room erupted into cheers and applause.

The full title of the document was "The Treaty of Peace and Amity between the United States of America and the Confederate States of America." Reagan and Black had taken the notes of the discussions taken by St. Martin and Williams, written out the text in a concise yet comprehensive manner, edited it back and forth a few times, and produced what all agreed was a very nice piece of work.

When he had first read through the final text, Breckinridge's heart had begun pounding. The treaty had marked the culmination of decades of political acrimony and nearly four years of bloody war. It would surely go down as one of the most historically significant documents in American history.

He was deeply disappointed, perhaps even bitter, that the treaty did not include his provision for the international military tribunal to prosecute those accused of atrocities. The lack of a referendum in Kentucky broke his heart. Still, he felt proud of the contribution he had made to the treaty negotiations. He knew, even if few others did, that the talks would have failed without his involvement. If the treaty had not been exactly what he had hoped for, it still marked the successful conclusion of the South's fight for independence. And that was worth celebrating.

The delegations had sent the final version of the treaty to Washington and Richmond on July 20. President McClellan's affirmtive response had arrived by telegram two days later. Three more anxious days of waiting followed. Breckinridge had feared that President Davis, stubborn and unrealistic as he so often was, would reject the treaty and demand a renegotiation for more favorable terms. Seymour had let it be known that they would pack up and go home if this happened. It had been a tremendous relief, then, when word of Davis's assent had finally come through the telegraph wires from Richmond.

As the applause died down, people quickly moved forward to crowd the delegates, all eager to shake hands and exchange a few words. Mayor Medcalf had had the foresight to arrange drinks and refreshments for the assembled spectators. Almost immediately, a festive atmosphere took hold of the room. All that was missing, Breckinridge thought wistfully, was music.

Stephens walked towards Breckinridge, smiling broadly, and extended his hand.

"We did it, John," he said. "I had my doubts for a time."

"As did I, Aleck. But we have succeeded. I think we can all be proud of the work we have done here in Toronto."

"Perhaps," Stephens said softly, taking a small sip from his champagne flute. "You know that there will be a lot of criticism when we get back home. We must be ready to weather the storm."

Breckinridge chuckled. "If I could face the fire of the Yankees at Murfreesboro and Chickamauga, I am prepared to face the scribbling of a few hostile newspaper editors."

"I sometimes wonder," Stephens said, before pausing awkwardly, as if uncertain whether to continue. "I sometimes wonder, John, whether we haven't committed the most dreadful folly."

"What do you mean?"

"Elections to Georgia's secession convention were held on January 2, 1861. It was a nail-biter, John. If only a thousand more votes had been cast for Unionist candidates, Georgia might not have seceded. And it had been a very rainy day in the northern part of the state, where support for secession was weakest."

Breckinridge nodded slowly. "And if Georgia had voted against secession, there probably would never have been a Confederacy."

"Precisely. Perhaps the old Union could have been preserved. I have thought about this many times, John, sometimes in despair. What if history will look back on us and declare us all fools?"

"It might," Breckinridge admitted.

"It doesn't matter though, does it? The die is cast, as Caesar said. We will have to sleep in the bed we have made."

Stephens smiled weakly and moved on to speak to some of the visitors. Breckinridge sipped his champagne and thought on the Vice President's words. He certainly understood the Stephens's pessimism, for he had also been devoutly attached to the Union before 1861. Yet he didn't share his doubts. The very moment they were living through was proof that the Confederacy had triumphed. How they would be viewed by history was a matter for future generations to worry about, not them.

He looked down at the two documents on the table again. They were nothing but pieces of paper which could be torn to shreds in a matter of seconds. Yet they represented the solemn agreement between the North and the South which, he devoutly hoped, would ensure peaceful and friendly relations between them for generations to come.

"Amazing, isn't it?" said Seymour, who had come up beside Breckinridge.

"What's that?"

"That it all comes down to those pieces of paper, I mean."

"I know. But that's the way it always is, isn't it? History explodes upon us and we think we can mold it into what we want. We can't. History happens to us. It isn't under our control. Then a few of us are left to pick up the pieces and try to put them back together into something that will not fall apart."

"Well, for what it's worth, I am honored to have served in these negotiations with you, John." The United States Secretary of State extended his hand, which Breckinridge took.

"It has been an honor on my part, too, Horatio."

"What will you do now?" Seymour asked. "A run for Congress?"

"From what state?" Breckinridge answered with a slightly bitter laugh. "You fellows have kept my native Kentucky out of the Confederacy." It obviously wouldn't be prudent for him to tell Seymour the truth.

"I'm sure you'll think of something," Seymour said with a grin. "We've established peace between the North and South, but it will be quite a task to maintain that peace. Frankly, I'd prefer the Confederacy be led by moderate men such as yourself." He cast a quick glance at Miles. "The alternatives are disquieting."

Breckinridge nodded knowingly and took another sip of his champagne. He realized he had drained the glass. Within a matter of seconds, Edmund was by his side.

"Another glass, sir?"

"Do you have any whiskey? Scotch, perhaps?"

"I could go and see, sir. It would take a few minutes."

"That's fine. Champagne is quite all right." He took a glass off the proffered tray with a smile.

Edmund scowled slightly. "I should hope so, sir. It's Taittinger." The Canadian valet moved on with his tray.

Breckinridge glanced through the room. Stephens and Seymour were both locked in a discussion with Mayor Medcalf and some other Canadian and British gentlemen Breckinridge did not recognize. Postmaster Reagan was seated by himself at the table, enjoying a cigar along with his champagne. Attorney General Black and Vice President Hamlin were talking off to the side of the main crowd, with Hamlin having an especially sour look on his face.

"Well, John? How do you feel?"

He turned to see Congressman Miles standing beside him, wearing his habitual smile and holding a glass of champagne in his hand.

"I am pleased, William. Very pleased. We have done quite well for ourselves."

"I'm glad you think so," Miles said, taking a sip from his glass. "I am very happy, too, but I do not think we are happy for the same reasons."

"Meaning what, William?"

Miles paused a moment before replying. "Well, I think you did what you came here to do and I did what I came here to do."

A feeling of alarm began to grow inside Breckinridge's heart. "I don't follow."

"No, you wouldn't follow, would you?"

Now Breckinridge was irritated. "I don't much enjoy games, Congressman. Speak plainly, if you please."

"Very well. I'll speak perfectly plainly." He glanced about the room, satisfying himself that no one else could hear their conversation over the din of the celebration. He then stared Breckinridge hard in the eye. "I know about your meeting with Hamlin. Going behind our backs to cut a deal with the enemy, John? Not the behavior of a Southern gentleman, I must say."

Breckinridge's blood turned to ice.

"What did Hamlin offer you, John?" Miles asked. "Money? A woman? Having trouble with your wife, John?"

"That was not what it was like at all," Breckinridge protested.

"The facts seem to indicate otherwise. You have a secret meeting at night with a member of the Union delegation and the next morning you are pushing the rest of us to drop the slavery provisions from our list of demands. You even gave up on the referendum in Kentucky. You, the Great Kentuckian, of all people!"

"How did you know about my meeting with Hamlin?"

"I was having you followed," Miles said nonchalantly, as though it were a matter of no concern.

"And you speak to me of being ungentlemanly, when you dared to have me followed?"

"Keep your voice down, John. I know what you have done. I do not think you wish the others to know. Besides, throwing a scene would ruin the celebration of this historic occasion."

165

Rage flared inside Breckinridge and he downed most of his champagne flute in a single gulp. "Explain yourself, sir," he said coldly.

Miles shrugged. "When you demonstrated a willingness to waver on the slavery issue, I thought it worthwhile to keep an eye on you. I figured you'd try to betray us at some point."

"I didn't betray anyone."

Miles ignored him and went on. "When I learned of the telegram sent by Senator Sumner to Hamlin, I expected him to reach out to you. It was an easy matter to hire a local ruffian to trail you."

His eyes narrowed in confusion. "How did you know about the telegram from Sumner?"

Miles chuckled slightly. "Are you a child, John? It doesn't cost much to bribe a telegraph operator."

Breckinridge had never considered bribing anyone in his life, much less a telegraph operator who was ostensibly duty bound to keep communications secret. Being a person of strict personal integrity himself, it was sometimes difficult to remember how unscrupulous other people could be. He silently berated himself for his naiveté. All his years in politics, to say nothing of his wartime experiences with Braxton Bragg, should have taught him how to recognize deviousness when he saw it.

"Why would you do this, William? We're on the same side."

"There you are wrong, my Kentucky friend. We are not on the same side. My side believes that we must defend the institution of slavery, even to the last extremity. My side believes that God Himself established the white man to rule over the black man and to make proper use of his labor. Anyone who is willing to compromise on that question, even in the slightest degree, is not on my side. You are not on my side, John."

"I serve the Confederacy, William."

"I really shouldn't have been surprised. How long did it take before you decided to join us, back in 1861? You were still sitting in the United States Senate after the true Confederates had fought bravely at Manassas. I think your reluctance to join the Confederacy speaks volumes about your character and loyalty."

Miles never stopped smiling while he spoke, nor did his tone become unfriendly. Somehow, this made his words all the more sinister.

The South Carolinian took another sip of champagne and continued. "Listen very carefully to what I'm about to tell you, John. I want you to burn these words into your soul. If you think you're going to be the next man to sit in Jeff Davis's chair, think again. Whoever is elected President in 1867 and 1873 and on until doomsday is going to be a man who believes in slavery and who will fight to the death to defend it. You're not that man, John."

"It's not up to you," Breckinridge said as sternly as he could. "It's up to the people."

"You've proven here in Toronto that you're willing to make deals with the damn Yankees. You're willing to let them get away with stealing the slave property of plantation owners. You're even willing to hand over your own state to the Yankees on a silver platter. When I look at you, I feel I might as well be looking at John Brown."

"What if I do run? What will you do to stop me?"

"Simple. I'll go to the newspapers. The *Richmond Examiner*. The *Charleston Mercury*. You name it. I'm sure they'd love to hear how the great John C. Breckinridge sold the South out at the treaty negotiations and how he loves to pal around with abolitionists. All of your popularity won't matter a damn once they learn what you have done. You saw how they treated old Pat Cleburne, didn't you?"

Breckinridge tensed at the words. He had served alongside Cleburne in the Army of Tennessee and had grown to respect the man immensely. He was perhaps the greatest soldier produced by the Confederacy, a true master of war. His brilliant defense of Atlanta in the face of Grant's assault had probably saved the Confederacy from total defeat in 1864. Yet when the newspapers had learned that Cleburne had authored a proposal to free the slaves and enlist them in the army, none of this had mattered. The Irishman had been excoriated in the press and denounced as an enemy of the Southern way of life. Despite the recommendations of Joseph Johnston, Robert E. Lee, and Breckinridge himself, the Confederate Senate had voted to reject Cleburne's promotion to the rank of Lieutenant General.

"You never intended for your slavery provisions to become part of the treaty," Breckinridge said. The full extent of Miles's deception was becoming clear, like the lifting of a fog.

"Of course not," Miles replied. "As you said many times, the Yankees would never have agreed to them. My aim from the very beginning was to make sure that you were the one who caved in to the Yankees on slavery, not me. When the story is told, I'll come out looking like the stalwart defender of the South, while you will come out looking like the traitorous weasel that you are."

168

"My future course will not be dictated by the likes of you, Miles."

"I'm holding a gun to your head, John. You told me that you were thinking of retiring from public life and resuming your law practice. I think that would be a very wise course of action. Because if you decide to seek public office again, I will destroy your reputation and ruin your career. I will make your children ashamed that you are their father and your wife ashamed that you are her husband. I will make lifelong friends of yours cross to the other side of the street to avoid having to exchange words with you. Your name will become synonymous with treason, just like old Benedict Arnold."

"You can't make that happen."

"Mark my words, John. I can make it happen. And if you run for office, I will make it happen." Miles tossed back the last of his champagne. "I seem to have emptied my glass. I shall get another. Would you like me to get another for you as well?"

"No, thank you," Breckinridge said automatically, his mind still trying to come to grips with everything Miles had just told him. The South Carolinian, his smile never wavering, moved off to find another glass of champagne.

Breckinridge had received many shocks in his life. He remembered the death of his beloved son John in 1850. He remembered how the Whigs and Know-Nothings had gerrymandered his congressional district in 1854 to force him out of the House of Representatives. He recalled the doomed assault of the Orphan Brigade at Murfreesboro, the tragic failure of Bragg to follow up the victory at Chickamauga, and the horrible moment when he had had to order the VMI boys into the line at New Market.

As he watched Congressman Miles happily take another champagne flute from Edmund's tray, Breckinridge realized that he had just experienced another such agonizing moment. In a way, it was the greatest and most frightening shock he had ever received in his life.

During his walk with Wolseley on the hills of the battlefield at Quebec, Breckinridge had decided that he would run for the presidency. He now knew that Miles would stand in his way, using his actions during the peace conference, especially his secret meeting with Hamlin, as his ammunition. The South Carolinian had the motive and the means to turn the wealthiest, most powerful, and most influential people in the Confederacy against him.

In a room filled with people, at what should have been one of the great triumphant moments of his life, John C. Breckinridge suddenly felt very much alone. The Bible said that peacemakers were blessed. He, for one, knew that this wasn't true. He was a peacemaker, yet he was cursed.

THE TREATY OF PEACE AND AMITY BETWEEN THE UNITED STATES OF AMERICA AND THE CONFEDERATE STATES OF AMERICA

The United States of America and the Confederate States of America, moved by a mutual and sincere desire to see the calamity of war and the unnecessary effusion of blood and treasure ended, and to establish peace on the firm foundations of friendship and mutual respect, have appointed for that purpose respective plenipotentiaries.

The President of the United States, the Honorable George McClellan, has appointed the following plenipotentiaries:

Horatio Seymour, Secretary of State of the United States

John Porter, Major General of the United States Army

Jeremiah Black, Attorney General of the United States

Hannibal Hamlin, Former Vice President of the United States

The President of the Confederate States, the Honorable Jefferson Davis, has appointed the following plenipotentiaries:

Alexander Stephens, Vice President of the Confederate States

John Breckinridge, Secretary of War of the Confederate States

William Miles, Member of the Confederate House of Representatives

John Reagan, Postmaster General of the Confederate States

These plenipotentiaries, after a reciprocal communication of their respective full powers, have arranged, agreed upon, and signed the following Treaty of Peace and Amity between the United States of America and the Confederate States of America.

Article I

There shall be a firm and universal peace between the United States and the Confederate States, and between their respective citizens, without any exception of places and persons. The two nations shall use their utmost efforts to preserve a perfect harmony between them and shall not permit any act of hostility whatever by sea or by land for any cause or under any pretext. Each nation shall avoid any act which might disturb the peace between them and neither nation shall give any assistance or protection, directly or indirectly, to any party or parties who wish to injure the other nation.

Article II

The United States acknowledges the full national sovereignty and political independence of the Confederate States.

Article III

Upon the exchange of mutual ratifications of this treaty, the military forces of the United States shall begin to withdraw from all territory of the Confederate States currently under their occupation, and the military forces of the Confederate States shall begin to withdraw from all territory of the United States currently under their occupation, with such withdrawal to be completed in as expedient a manner as practical, but within three months in any event. Care shall be taken to avoid unnecessary disruptions to civilians and there shall be no destruction of property during this time.

Article IV

Immediately upon the exchange of mutual ratifications of this treaty, the United States and the Confederate States shall transmit orders to their respective naval vessels, wherever they might be, to immediately cease all hostile action against the other party. Furthermore, immediately upon the exchange of mutual ratifications of this treaty, the United States shall lift the naval blockade imposed upon the Confederate States on April 19, 1861.

Article V

All prisoners taken by either side, on land or sea, without regard to race or previous condition of servitude, shall be restored within three months of the exchange of mutual ratifications of this treaty.

Article VI

The territory of the Confederate States of America consists of the following states: Virginia (excepting those counties ceded to the United States as specified in Article X), North Carolina, South Carolina, Georgia, Florida, Alabama, Mississippi, Arkansas and Texas. The status of Louisiana and Tennessee shall be determined by the result of plebiscites as specified in Article IX.

Article VII

Military posts, forts, and other government facilities that belonged to the United States government within the confines of a state on the date of that state's secession from the United States shall devolve to the Confederate States.

Article VIII

The Confederate States forever repudiates any and all territorial claims to the State of Maryland, the State of West Virginia, the State of Kentucky, the State of Missouri, the Territory of New Mexico, the Indian Territory, and any portions thereof.

Article IX

Plebiscites shall be held in the states of Louisiana and Tennessee to enable their citizens to decide for themselves whether their states shall become a part of the United States or the Confederate States. Immediately upon the exchange of mutual ratifications of this treaty, the United States and the Confederates States shall each appoint, for each state, five commissioners to create a ten-person commission with authority to organize and oversee the plebiscites within Louisiana and Tennessee and to ensure that the elections be free and fair. The plebiscites shall be held within one year of the exchange of mutual ratifications of this treaty.

Article X

The following counties of Virginia are ceded to the United States: Fairfax, Loudoun, and Alexandria.

Article XI

Each party reserves to itself the right to fortify whatever point within its territory it may judge proper so to fortify for its security.

Article XII

The United States and the Confederate States agree that the Indian Territory shall be an independent state under the mutual supervision and protection of both powers. Negotiations for establishing a proper government in the Indian Territory shall commence not less than six months after the mutual exchange of ratifications of this treaty.

Article XIII

Persons whose property was damaged or destroyed by military forces of the United States or the Confederate States during the course of the late war, and who maintain that said damage or destruction was not warranted by military necessity, shall be permitted to file suit against the offending party for financial restitution.

Article XIV

Persons who were held to servitude under the laws of the Confederate States and were set at liberty by the military forces of the United States during the late war and have since relocated to the United States are hereby granted the legal status of free individuals. Claims of ownership of such individuals by citizens of the Confederate States are absolutely null and void.

Article XV

When traveling into the United States, citizens of the Confederate States shall not be permitted to bring persons held to servitude under the laws of the Confederate States with them.

Article XVI

The vessels and citizens of the United States shall, in all time, have free, unhindered and uninterrupted use of the Mississippi River for means of transportation, armed vessels of a military nature alone excepted. In the Confederate ports on the Mississippi River, citizens of the United States shall enjoy the same rights and privileges on matters of deposit and harbor fees as citizens of the Confederate States.

Article XVII

The citizens of the United States and the Confederate States shall have the freedom to trade in the territory of the other nation and shall pay within the other nation no other or greater duties, charges or fees whatsoever than the most-favored-nations are or shall be obliged to pay; and they shall enjoy all the rights, privileges and exemptions in navigation and commerce, which the most-favored-nation does or shall enjoy; submitting themselves nevertheless to the laws and usages there established, and to which are submitted the citizens and subjects of the most-favored-nations.

Article XVIII

To facilitate commerce and friendly relations, the two nations grant to each other the liberty of having in the ports or inland centers of commerce of the other consuls, vice-consuls, agents & commissaries of their own appointment, whose functions shall be regulated by particular agreement whenever either party shall choose to make such appointment; but if any such consuls shall exercise commerce, they shall be submitted to the same laws and usages to which the private individuals of their nation are submitted in the same place.

Article XIX

The United States and the Confederate States, on requisitions made in their name through the medium of their respective diplomatic or consular agents, shall deliver up to justice such persons who, being charged with murder, attempt to commit murder, rape, forgery, arson, robbery, or embezzlement, committed within the jurisdiction of the requiring party, shall be found within the territories of the other, provided that this shall be done only when the fact of the commission of the crime shall be so established as to justify their apprehension and commitment for trial if the crime had been committed in the country where the persons so accused shall be found. The expense of the detention and delivery shall be at the cost of the party making the demand.

Article XX

Vessels of one nation that are legally in the jurisdiction of the other nation shall be subject to the same rules, regulations and protections as are extended to the vessels of the other nation, but vessels belonging to a citizen of the United States or flying the flag of the United States shall not be permitted to transport persons held to servitude under any circumstances. When any vessel of either nation shall be wrecked, foundered, or otherwise damaged within the jurisdiction of the other, the crew and vessel shall receive the same assistance which would be due to the citizens of the nation in which the incident takes place.

Article XXI

If private citizens of either nation, acting under proper law, shall erect monuments or memorials to their respective war dead on battlefields in the territory of the other nation, the local authorities shall protect said monuments and memorials and treat any act of vandalism directed towards them as a serious criminal offense.

Article XXII

Both nations agree that creditors on either side shall face no legal impediment to the full recovery of any legitimate debts they may have accrued before the separation of the United States and Confederate States, legislation passed by either government in the interim notwithstanding.

Article XXIII

One third of the United States national debt as of January 1, 1861, shall be assumed by the Confederate States.

Article XXIV

There shall be no confiscation made nor any prosecutions commenced against any person or persons for, or by reason of, the part which he or they may have played in the late war. No person shall on that account suffer any loss or damage, either in his person, liberty, or property. Those who may be in confinement on such charges at the time of the ratification of this treaty shall immediately be set at liberty and the prosecutions so commenced shall be discontinued.

Article XXV

If any dispute should hereafter arise between the United States and the Confederate States, the two nations honestly pledge to one another that they will endeavor to settle their differences, and to preserve the state of peace and friendship in which the two countries are now placing themselves, through peaceful negotiations.

Article XXVI

If unhappily war should ever again arise between the two nations, the citizens of either nation then residing in the other shall be allowed to remain six months to collect their debts and settle their affairs, and may depart freely, carrying off all their effects, without molestation or hindrance.

CONCLUDED IN TORONTO, CANADA, JULY 25, 1865. RATIFIED BY THE UNITED STATES ON SEPTEMBER 1, 1865, AND THE CONFEDERATE STATES ON SEPTEMBER 6, 1865. RATIFICATIONS EXCHANGED AT CITY POINT, VIRGINIA, ON SEPTEMBER 8, 1865.

About the Author

Jeff Brooks was born in Richmond, Virginia, and grew up in Dallas, Texas. He currently lives in Manor, Texas, just outside the state capital of Austin. He graduated from Texas State University with a double bachelor's degree in history and political science and a master's degree in history. He also studied at the University of Kent in Canterbury, England. Aside from his writing, he teaches life skills to students with special needs at Anderson High School. He is a certified wine sommelier and a devoted fan of Chelsea Football Club.

Jeff met his lovely wife Jill at a wine tasting in 2009. They married in the Bahamas in 2011. In 2013, their daughter Evelyn was born.

Shattered Nation: An Alternate History Novel of the American Civil War was Jeff's first book. It was published in 2013. *Blessed are the Peacemakers* is Jeff's second book.

Made in United States
North Haven, CT
03 February 2024

48300868R00104